STILL *You*

AMY K. MCCLUNG

HOT TREE PUBLISHING

STILL YOU

AMY K. MCCLUNG

HOT TREE PUBLISHING

ALSO BY AMY K. MCCLUNG

STAND-ALONES

STILL YOU

A LITTLE SPARK

ACROSS THE WAY

FINDING YOUR WAY

THE SOUTHERN DEVOTION SERIES

FOR THE LOVE OF GRACIE

CURVES IN THE ROAD

COMPLICATED RELATIONSHIPS

TWISTED FATE

COMPLETE BOX SET

For information, contact the publisher, Hot Tree Publishing.

Cover updated: 2021

www.hottreepublishing.com

Editor: Hot Tree Editing

E-book: 978-1-925448-69-6

Paperback: 978-1-925448-81-8

To my best friend and husband, Daniel, who inspires every romantic moment I write.

CHAPTER 1
EDEN

I'D SPENT THE PAST THREE YEARS ON MY KNEES, FACE DEEP in bush. It wasn't as sexy as it sounded; I owned a landscaping company called Gardens of Eden. "Company" sounded bigger than it was, too. I was the founder, CEO, President, and the only employee of said company. After doing the whole four-year-college thing, getting my degree in accounting, and spending six years working dead-end jobs hoping to find one in my major, I decided to put my skills to work for me. Living in a condo, I didn't have any gardening to do at home. My sister, Eve, however, had a black thumb, and what started with me appeasing my own horror at seeing her eyesore of a yard turned into a business idea. With the way weather went in Nashville, landscaping was almost a year-round job. In reality, it was at least seven or eight months of work, starting as early as April and ending as late as November. For the other few months, I had another job to supplement my income.

Turning into the new subdivision I recently scored a contract for, I glanced down at my logbook to check the address one more time. The neighborhood was more upscale than I was used to, but the address checked out. On my first day at a new house, I never scheduled anyone else. It gave me a chance to see how much work needed to be done and get the yard ready so that every other visit could fit into a schedule of one to two hours at most.

Stepping out of my truck, I pulled the clipboard from the console and strolled up the walkway to the front door. Before I could knock, the door swung open and a young girl of about four let out a high-pitched scream, causing every dog in the neighborhood to howl.

"Kid… hey, kid…." The more I talked, the more the girl screamed. Nothing would cry "stranger danger" more than if I picked her up and covered her mouth right now. Just as I was about to turn and run for the hills, I saw a flash of abs headed straight for the door. Muscular arms scooped up the shrieking nightmare child. He turned to the side, and I spotted a tattoo of a dragon wrapped around the bulging bicep currently holding up the now giggling girl. Dark, black hair fell framing his face, and his bare chest had a light smattering of matching curl. Damn if I wasn't having completely dirty thoughts as I stared at the glorious man in front of me.

"I'm sorry about little stink here. She's been taught not to talk to strangers, and we haven't quite gotten down the correct response. Mom thought it would be enough to tell her to scream, but now most of us don't have the hearing we used to because she screams at the UPS guy, the mailman, the neighbor, and now apparently...." Glancing around me, he spotted my truck. "Gardens of Eden? Are you a stripper?"

I coughed in surprise before my voice cracked with embarrassment. "No." I cleared my throat and manned up my voice a bit. "No, I'm here to trim the bushes, mow the yard, and take care of any plants. At least that's what my invoice says. I'm sorry, is Maggie here? She's the name I have on my list."

"Mags!" sexy bulging bicep god called. "Your stripper's here!" Watching him snicker at his lame attempt at a joke, I groaned, wishing I hadn't gone for the cutesy name on my truck.

"What are you screaming about, Adam?" A stunning redhead wearing a business suit was struggling to come down the stairs as she put on her heels at the same time. She sized me up, a grin forming on her face. "Are you Eden?" I nodded, and she continued, "Come inside, please. Adam, this is the new landscaper." She pointed her index finger at him and said to me, "Ignore him. He provides the bank account, and I pay the bills. It's a wonderful union we have." She winked. I offered her a smile and cleared my throat nervously once more.

Inside, the house was even more immaculate than the outside, no doubt decorated by the striking Maggie. Nothing over the top, no furniture seeming more for display than sitting, but everything in its place. Above the ivory-colored marble fireplace hung a portrait of the shrieking child with an older boy and girl. Each child appeared plucked from a modeling catalog. As my gaze moved back over the couple, lingering too long on Adam's body, I sighed, wondering what it must be like to have the perfect life.

There was no time for daydreaming. Instead, I started my usual spiel. "Since today is my first visit, I offer a satisfaction guarantee. If you aren't happy with how it looks, it will be no charge." Flipping through my notes from our phone conversation, I tried to decipher my own scribble and made a mental note to take time at night to type these out. "You wanted the grass cut today as well as some pruning done on your bush? Just one?" Adam cleared his throat and Maggie not so subtly jabbed him in the chest with her elbow.

"One set in particular needs the most work, but you

can trim all of them up. On the right side of the house the set of bushes looks—"

"Obscene?" Adam offered, again receiving a jab from Maggie's elbow. He chuckled as his face scrunched up and he rubbed the now sore spot.

Maggie sighed. "Amber loves animals, and I thought I could form the bushes into animal shapes. I tried for a giraffe and elephant."

"Instead, it looks like a dwarf swinging a sword at a horny giant."

Trying to stifle my laughter, I made a note to check the right side of the house.

Ignoring Adam's comment, Maggie continued giving directions for her yard work. "Now, when you come back I may want a bit of landscaping done in the front yard. My husband planted a few things out there, but I've never been a green thumb, and Adam and I don't have time to keep it up."

"We can talk about it once I'm done today. If you're happy with the job, I'll schedule you for the land-scaping as well. Here is my card." Reaching into my wallet, I pulled out my business card, mentally groaning again at the cute name. *Why did I let my sister talk me into that name?*

"Sounds great. I need to get to work. Adam is home today, so when you get done, or if you have any ques-tions, see him. I trust his judgment. Nice to meet you,

Eden." Her hand, though soft, gripped mine firmly. By her demeanor, the businesslike tone of her voice, and the way she presented herself, I could tell she was in a position of authority in whatever business she was in.

Adam followed her to the door and gave her a kiss on the cheek. "Enjoy your day, honey. See you tonight." When she turned around, he gave her a backhanded pop on the bottom, sending her off with a squeak and a giggle. From the outside looking in, they seemed to be the perfect couple.

Once we were alone, Adam's gaze raked over me, making me a little uncomfortable but also a bit turned on. *Could I have been mistaken about his sexuality?*

CHAPTER 2
ADAM

Leaving me as the lone adult in the house, Eden went to start his work on the front yard. With my laptop open on the kitchen table, I sat down to log in. I'd been working nights while Maggie worked days so we could avoid paying for childcare. I glanced at my Facebook page, but grew bored of the constant back and forth of political memes and taunts. Sighing, I realized I needed something more productive to do during my downtime at home.

The low hum of a weed eater caught my attention, so I strolled over to the window to check on the gardener. My breath caught in my throat as I took in his appearance. When he came into the house, he'd been in a button-down shirt tucked into jeans with his hair slicked back in a businesslike manner. The summer heat of Nashville was at a miserable ninety-eight with a heat index of 106, so he'd stripped out of the shirt, leaving only a white tank that now stuck to his skin with sweat. His slicked-back blond hair had fallen around his face as the sweat loosened whatever product he'd used. Pausing momentarily, he swiped his thick forearm across his brow, removing as much sweat as he could. My cock strained against my pants while I admired his form. Watching him grab a do-rag from his back pocket and dab it across his forehead before wrapping it around his hair, all I could think of was using it to tie his hands to the bed while I had my way with him.

"Uncle Adam." A small, sweet voice rang out, scaring the shit out of me.

"Little stink. I thought you were taking a nap." Rubbing her eyes, she stepped closer to me. Considering all the thoughts running through my head about the gardener, I wished she were anywhere but here.

"I want to watch *Fwozen*."

"Again? Kid, you gotta let it go." She giggled at my terrible pun. Giggles from Amber were my favorite thing to hear. At four, she was the youngest of her siblings, just behind Gideon, who was six, and Jordan, age eight. "Come on, we'll set you up in the living room."

After setting up the DVD player and getting her snuggled into a couch full of pillows, I made sure the front door was locked and removed the key so Amber couldn't go outside without me knowing. Strolling back into the kitchen, I stopped in my tracks as the sexy gardener stood in front of the window with his tank top raised enough to give a glimpse of his rock-hard abs. *Fuck.* The man was losing all the water in his body, and all I wanted to do was watch him wash the grime off and see water cascade over those taut fucking abs.

I grabbed a water bottle from the fridge, then opened the back door and whistled to get Eden's attention. "Want some water, man? You look like you've lost yours." Eden cocked his eyebrow at my rather lame joke. It made me wonder for a moment what his full name was. And I needed to tone back the immaturity a bit with him. Maggie and I acted like kids when we were together, but I didn't want to look like a complete tool around this man.

"Thanks, I appreciate it. I usually keep a cooler in my truck, but I was running late this morning and forgot it." He raised the bottle, and I watched with awe as he wrapped his beautiful pink lips around the opening, mesmerized as his Adam's apple bobbed up and down as he drank. *Adam's apple?* Fuck yeah, I could totally claim him right now and devour him like a sweet, succulent apple. *Damn.* It'd been too long since I'd had sex.

Taking a look around at the work he'd done, I was amazed at how different the yard looked in comparison to the last time I tried to fix it up for Maggie. "I'm positive Mags is going to want you back. It looks amazing out here. Did you do that?" I pointed toward a birdbath in the yard, previously covered in filth with weeds grown all around it, now gleaming in the sun with fresh water and surrounded by tiny purple flowers.

"The flowers were there, but I did take a moment to clean up the birdbath and trim around it. It wasn't part of the plan today, but it was driving me crazy to have an eyesore with my awesome landscaping around it." Eden threw a wink my way, and it made me blush like a thirteen-year-old girl. "I'm done out here. Since I have your approval, do you mind if I get the check and head on?"

"Oh, yeah. I'll be right back." I ran into the house, grabbed Maggie's checkbook and ripped the check out, turned around, and stopped in my tracks. "Fuck me." Eden had taken the rest of the bottle of water and dumped it over his head to cool himself off. When had my yard become an episode of *Baywatch*? It took me back to when I first knew I was attracted to men, watching reruns of *Baywatch*. Seeing David Hasselhoff running down the beach was more exciting than Pam Anderson's boobs bouncing down it.

I gazed dumbstruck out the window, my eyes glued to his body, following each trail of water gliding down his slick skin. My hands gripped the back of the kitchen chair in front of me until my knuckles were white. Eden's eyes met mine, and as I scrambled away to hide the fact I'd been staring, I fell to the floor.

<h1 style="text-align:center">CHAPTER 3
EDEN</h1>

IF I HADN'T KNOWN BETTER, I WOULD HAVE THOUGHT Adam had been checking me out through the window. One minute I spotted him staring, and the next he disappeared. Appearing at the back door, he brought me my payment, eyes raking over me once more. After seeing him with Maggie, though, I couldn't imagine him ever being gay.

It'd never been easy for me to spot someone safe to ask out. For the first few years of puberty, I dated girls and wondered why I didn't have these crazy, lustful feelings for them like I saw on television or in movies.

My sister, Eve, was the one who finally convinced me to give a guy a chance. Two years older than me, she graduated at the end of my sophomore year. Just before she left for college, we had a nice long chat where she suggested it was time for me to come out.

You could've knocked me over with a feather because I'd never even hinted to her about any attraction toward men. Then again, she always knew me better than I knew myself.

Once I admitted it to Eve, she often urged me to free myself by coming out. For two years after, I stressed over telling my parents—uber-religious Catholics who never missed a holy day and attended church more than they watched television. Even when we went on trips, if it fell during the holy days, we had to locate a nearby Catholic church to attend service. As we got older, they let my sister and me slide on the holy days, but we still had to attend on the Sabbath, or at least Saturday night service. As much as I worried over telling them, the final result went much smoother than I expected and they'd never been anything but supportive. Rarely did I take a guy home to meet them, but when I did, they welcomed him with open arms.

It had been a long time since someone had captured my attention the way Adam had today. Adam—his name was biblical as well, which was either a sign we were meant to be together or a warning to run for my life. The thought of us as a couple, Adam and Eden, was laughable. We might as well be the old cliché of Adam and Steve that bible thumpers ridiculed.

Referring to us "we" seemed presumptuous, especially when all signs pointed to Adam being straight and married. It was a nice fantasy, though.

Maggie called me later in the evening to thank me for such a wonderful job. She signed up for biweekly service and contracted me to do a complete makeover of her front yard. Each time I got a new yard contract it was a good feeling, proof my business was going strong. For this one, it was even more satisfying knowing I'd get to see Adam again.

My first stop the next day was at Eve's house. "Hello? Eve? Jackie?" I called out after entering the front door. I had my own key, so I let myself in on the days I worked on my sister's yard. She always left me something for lunch and plenty of water to drink, whether she'd be home or not.

Peering around the corner, Eve pointed at the phone in her hand and mouthed, "One more minute, I promise." Out loud she said, "Yes, Mark, the documentation is there. I had the parents sign off yesterday, so everything should be ready for the court date." Pausing a moment, she rolled her eyes. "Look, I'll come down in a bit. My brother is on his way here. I'll see if he can sit with my daughter while I come help you look." Eve peered at me with puppy dog eyes and a pouty lip. Wrapped around her little finger was where I'd been most of my life.

Finally hanging up the phone, she sighed. "Jackie's

got a cold, so she's home from school. I have an adoption going down tomorrow and Mark can't find the paperwork. If you could sit with her for an hour, tops, I'd be able to find it."

"It's fine, sis. If you want to go now, you can."

"Nope, I started a pizza and I want to sit down and eat with my brother. So, sit." Following her orders, I took a seat at the table while she pulled a steaming-hot vegetable pizza out of the oven and fixed us each a plate.

"How's work?" Cheese strung from her lips to the slice of pizza in her hand.

"Great. I scored a couple of new contracts in a subdivision in Brentwood. I worked on one house and the woman loved me and referred me to two of her neighbors." Cringing at the sour taste of the lemonade, I grabbed a sugar packet from the bowl on her table.

"That's amazing!"

"It's not a bad gig either. There's a guy that lives there—I'm not completely sure of their relationship, but I think they're married. He's been stuck in my mind since that day though. I caught him looking at me a few times."

Suddenly interested in what I'd say next, she leaned forward with her chin on her hand. With a mischievous grin, she asked, "Is he hot?"

"Scorching. I haven't been so turned on by a man in

a long time, sis." It was true. The last long-term relationship I had was in college, five years ago, and since then it'd been a date or two set up by friends. "I go back in a week, and all I can think about is seeing him again. How stupid does that sound?"

"Why does it sound stupid?" Her forehead was creased with confusion.

"The man is a client. I should be more professional." It was an unspoken rule not to dip in the company pool. He didn't work for me, but I worked for him, which made it seem weird.

"Making friends doesn't make you unprofessional. Next time you're there, talk to him. See what you might have in common. You may be misinterpreting their relationship."

Maybe Eve was right. I'd take her advice. For the next week, I would think about how to approach a conversation with him.

CHAPTER 4
ADAM

Maggie had forgotten to mention, or I'd forgotten to remember, that Eden was coming by today. So when the doorbell rang, I shuffled over in Maggie's high heels—the open-toed variety with my toes spilling over the edge—with a crown on my forehead. I opened the door, and Eden's gaze washed over me. "Am I interrupting something, princess?"

"I'm the queen. Amber is a princess. It's tea time, care for a cup?" His eyes followed the sway of my arm to see our table set up in the living room with a Disney tea set. Amber had on a crown and high heels as well. We had a set date for tea time once a week, but I would've rescheduled had I known it fell at the time Eden was coming by. Then again, Amber had me wrapped around her finger, so I probably wouldn't have.

"I'd love a cup, but I need to get to work. Rain check?" Amber gave him a funny look so I took a moment to explain.

"He'll have one later, little stink. Keep mine hot for a moment please." I kicked off my heels and dropped the crown on the chair. "Follow me, Eden." In the kitchen, I grabbed the list from Maggie off the fridge. "Maggie was thrilled about your work last time, which is good. So this time she added more things she wants and is prepared for any cost associated. In other words, I'm going to pay you any extra for what she wants."

He glanced over the list for a moment, nodding here and there, occasionally cocking an eyebrow. "She wants me to clear out space to build in a small garden? If she wants raised beds, I can build it for her as well instead of simply getting the space ready. In my off season, I do carpentry work. I'll jot down a few notes while I'm here and send her a quote. She can shop around as well, of course, and let me know."

"Sounds good. I have a feeling she won't shop around. She's quite pleased with you. Our neighbors are convinced you're a relative, what with how much she boasts about you." As he made a few notes on his clipboard, he smiled. He was a beautiful man. "I'm going to go back to check on Amber. If you need anything, just come in the back door and call out." And with a nod, Eden was out the door.

Amber had plopped herself down on the couch and gotten lost in the cartoon on the television. "Kiddo, you want to go play outside for a little bit?"

"Yes!" Amber jumped up and began bouncing up and down excitedly.

"Grab your tennis shoes and let's go!" As soon as she ran her shoes over to me, I slipped them on and showed her the bunny loop to tie them. We hadn't quite gotten her to learn the trick, but she always recited the words with me as I showed her.

One side of the yard had a playground set up for the kids. It was out of Eden's way, so we wouldn't bother him, but I had a great view of him as he worked. Amber ran up the ladder, slid down screaming, ran back around to the ladder, and repeated. At this rate, she'd tire herself out just in time for a midday nap. While Amber played, I pulled up an app on my phone to watch the latest episode of *Supernatural*. As sexy as Sam and Dean were, I watched mostly for the paranormal aspect... mostly.

Just as the opening music began, Eden walked over. "I love that song. It's the theme for one of my favorite shows." I turned the screen around to show him the video playing, and he grinned widely. "You're a fan?"

"Hell yeah. Seen every episode. Well, there's one I have never and will never watch." Shivers crept across my skin at the very thought.

"Let me guess, season one? Bugs?" Considering his job, Eden would most likely think I was a terrible wuss for being creeped out by bugs.

With my hand over my eyes to shield the embarrassment, I squeaked out, "Yep. Go ahead, make fun of me."

"No, man, it's cool. My sister refused to watch it as well. Actually, she watched it like this." Eden placed his hands over his eyes and spread two fingers apart just enough to see through the slit. Pointing to the seat next to me, he asked, "Do you mind?"

"No, please sit." I moved over a little to give him more room. Also, it helped me keep my cool if I kept a bit of room between us. "Do you have a favorite scene?"

"Wow, only about fifty. But I would say Castiel talking about the pizza man is high up there. As for episodes, the one where Dean is afraid of everything is a classic." It was as though we were kindred spirits. He'd picked out two things that stood out most to me when *Supernatural* was mentioned.

"Those, and of course, pudding." Eden held up his fist for me, and I bumped it with mine. "Whenever I watch the pudding scene, I rewind it at least three times. Mags and I binge watch it on a regular basis. Between that show and *The Walking Dead*, I'm not sure how we ever have time for anything else."

Eden crossed one leg over the other, shifting his body toward mine on the swing. "Another great show. Most episodes are depressing or downright devastating, but it's like crack. I can't get enough of it."

Momentarily distracted from the conversation, I noticed Amber still running in circles around the slide, going up the ladder, down the slide, again and again. "Little stink, slow down. Take a minute to swing and relax, please." I mumbled, "Sheesh, I wish I had half the energy she does."

"No kidding. I watch my niece, Jackie, when Eve needs me to. She runs circles around me." Eden stared at Amber for a few minutes before he reached into his pocket and pulled out a small notepad. "How old is this swing set?"

"No clue. It was here with the house, so it's older than ten years. Why?"

"I built one for Jackie one year, and she loved it." As he spoke, he scribbled something on the paper. "It's got swings, a tire swing, a slide, monkey bars, and it's shaped like a castle with a turret on either side." Palm out with the notepad on top, he showed me what he'd been drawing. It was a sketch of what he'd just described to me.

"Amber would love something to call her castle." Leaning down, I whispered, "She thinks she's a real princess, and we don't have the heart to tell her differently." The smile on Eden's face showed me he understood the need for playing along with little girls' dreams. I guessed his niece had him whipped. "Can I keep the sketch to show Mags?"

Eden ripped the paper from his pad, folded it in half, and handed it over. Our hands grazed. His were rough and calloused, demonstrating how much he worked with them. Woodworking, I imagined, would put the biggest toll on your hands. "I'll talk to her about it before your next trip over here."

"Guess I should get back to work." When he stood up, I grabbed his hand. His gaze drifted down to the connection and I let go.

"You could sit a few more minutes, can't you?" During the day, I had no one but a child to interact with. In the evenings, I would share a quick bite with Maggie before going to work. And at work, I was on my feet running around stressed for most of the time. It would be nice to sit and have a conversation with an adult for a few minutes.

"Looks like your princess is ready for a nap." Eden directed my attention to the swing, where Amber had laid her head against the chain. She was so exhausted from running laps around the playground, her head fell to my shoulder as soon as I lifted her into my arms. "Rain check on the talk too?"

"If you finish up and have nowhere to be, you

could come inside and talk for a bit. While she sleeps, I'll just be in the kitchen staring blankly at Facebook, wondering what there was to do before social media." All of this was whispered to keep from waking Amber. Eden gave me a thumbs-up.

A light knock on the door came about thirty minutes later. Peering up from my laptop, I smiled at the quick glimpse of Eden straightening his hair. I'd left the door unlocked, so I waved him in. "She's upstairs in bed, so we don't have to be extra quiet."

"You weren't kidding. You're staring at Facebook?" Sliding into the chair next to me, Eden tried peering at my page.

"You know you want to send me a friend request." Reaching over, he typed something in my search bar. A moment later, it popped up to show his business page. "Liked," I said, hitting the button.

"Have Maggie look it over later. There are examples on here of gardens I've done and a few of my carpentry projects as well."

"Will do." I closed my laptop, wanting to keep from getting into a business discussion. "Would you like a drink?" When Eden stalled with a few ums, I realized how my question sounded. "Nonalcoholic, of course. We have lemonade, sweet tea, and water. Maggie doesn't like to have soda in the house."

"Sweet tea would be great." While I filled glasses

with ice cubes and poured the tea, Eden flipped through a book on the table. "You read?" Eden frowned, clearly insulted at my phrasing. I clarified my question. "Do you like to read is what I mean."

"I do. I'm a Stephen King fan. Saw him at the Ryman last year. Is this yours?" It was a copy of a paranormal story I'd just finished reading.

"Mags saw it advertised on Facebook and bought a copy for me. It's got some great lines in it. If you'd like to borrow it, go ahead. I'll want it back though." With a grin, I set his tea down in front of him with a plastic bottle of lemon juice.

"Thanks. I'll get it back to you next time I'm here." Bringing the glass up to his lips, Eden took a long swig. He licked his lips as he set the cup back on the table. "Perfect tea." After another sip, he asked, "What do you do for a living?"

From the other room, tiny footsteps could be heard running across the hardwood floor. "Amber must have woken. Excuse me for a moment." She must have been up for a few minutes because the living room had toys everywhere and there were crayons on the table. Not just sitting on the table, but drawn all over the wood. "Sh… sugar." I stopped myself from cursing in front of the kid. "Your mom is going to kick my butt."

I snatched her up in my arms; she wriggled around, giggling, as I hauled her into the kitchen. Eden raised an eyebrow. "I thought she was taking a nap. She sounds like she's hopped up on sugar."

"Tell me about it. I think she got into my stash of chocolate upstairs. She's drawn a masterpiece all over the coffee table in there. I need to clean it up."

Eden rose from the table. "Thanks for the drink and the reading material." He held up the book. "I'll return this when I come back for my next job. Give me a call if Maggie decides she wants to go ahead with those projects we discussed."

When Eden left, I kicked myself for not getting to know more about him. We'd spent most of our time together as a business pitch. I could tell by the glances he'd sent my way that he was attracted to me as much as I was to him. The way he talked, though, was all business. Maybe next time I'd be able to persuade him to get a little more personal with me.

CHAPTER 5
EDEN

I had my moment with Adam, the chance to find out if he was interested in me, and I spent the entire time giving him a sales pitch. Why did I have such a hard time flirting?

My next client had canceled for the day. If I had seen the message in time, I might have offered to stay and help him clean up.

Sitting at home, I rehashed all the stupid missed moments of the day. Trying to erase it all from my mind, I picked up the book he'd recommended. I was immediately sucked into the story, and two hours passed by in a blink as I finished it.

My computer sat in the corner of the room on a small desk. I logged in to Facebook to check on my business page. Occasionally I got a message or a comment on the page, wanting pricing information.

Today I had three messages. One was from Adam, which I recognized from his profile picture, so I clicked on it first. He'd written, "I forgot to give you my phone number. In case you can't get in touch with Maggie sometime, here is another number you can try. And feel free to text me when you're done with the book."

It was an open invitation to contact him, and I wouldn't let it go to waste.

Me: Finished the book. You were right, it was a great read.

Adam: Damn! How'd you have time to get through it so quick?

Me: After I left your place, my last client canceled. Came straight home.

Adam: That sucks. It's too bad you couldn't have hung out more.

Me: I thought the same thing. Maybe next time.

Adam: Definitely.

No matter how many jobs I scheduled or how many men I met, I couldn't get Adam out of my head. It was a good thing I always took great notes on what people wanted, because if I had to remember anything else other than Adam's firm jaw, or his pale pink lips, the way his cheeks dimpled when he smiled, or the soft feel of his hands, I'd be in trouble. Working on a yard in Adam's neighborhood, I became distracted when I noticed him out in the yard with Amber.

Shirtless, wearing only a pair of gray shorts, he chased Amber around the yard with a hose. From two doors down, I could hear her shrieking with joy instead of fear for a change. It was a much more pleasant sound.

Lost in watching him play with his daughter, I had no clue how much time went by. Adam spotted me and waved. Lifting Amber up in his arms, he started walking across the yards toward me. I swiped away sweat and pushed my hair back, hoping to look presentable at least. Looking in a mirror right now was the last thing I'd have wanted to do. Imagining my face was clean and my hair perfect seemed to be easier on my ego.

"Hey, man." Adam grinned widely. "I assumed you'd do all the yards in this neighborhood on the same day."

"I tried to set it up that way, but Mr. Williams needed Tuesdays instead of Thursdays. It's fine though. I was going to bring your book by after I finished. It's in my van." Adam's grin grew wider.

"I'm off work tonight. Would you want to hang out for a bit? I'd love the adult company for the day." Giving Amber a kiss on the cheek, he said, "No offense, little stink."

"Sure, I can come over when I finish. If you don't mind the stench."

Without hesitation, Adam offered, "You could take a shower at the house."

Only if you take one with me. I held that back.

"That was probably a weird thing to offer. I have Febreze if you want to use it. It's what I use when I run out of laundry."

"Seriously?"

He chuckled. "I'm joking. I've heard of it being done though." I was sure he'd just backtracked to save face. "What time will you be done?"

The yard was almost finished. All I had left to do was trim the bushes around the back of the house. "About an hour?"

"Come on over to the house. Front door will be open. I'll get this one in bed, so don't ring the doorbell or knock. Just come on in. See you then." I watched him walk back toward his house, hating to see him go but loving to watch him leave.

An hour later, I stood in his doorway, peering inside. It seemed awkward to be in the living room all filthy. Sitting on the table was a towel and a note. "Downstairs bedroom is open if you want to grab a shower. I'll be down in a bit."

"Why not," I mumbled. Pulling my shirt up to my nose, I gagged. "Shower isn't going to help the smell of my clothes." Running back out to my van, I grabbed my gym bag from the back seat. I hadn't been to the gym this week, so I had clean clothes to wear.

The downstairs bathroom was exquisite, with marble countertops, a freestanding shower the size of my bathroom at home, and a large garden tub in the opposite corner.

With the water set to scalding, I stepped under the spray, allowing it to wash away as much of the dirt as possible. The soap in the shower hadn't been opened, so I made a mental note to buy them a replacement. Based on how clean and untouched this room and bathroom were, I assumed it was a guest bedroom. Made me curious what the regular bedrooms looked like when this one was so decked out.

I was startled by a knock on the door, followed by a voice calling out, "Eden?"

"Yeah!" I yelled over the sound of the water.

"I'm going to make a snack. You like chips and salsa, or queso?" It was difficult to concentrate on the question when I wanted Adam to fling the door open, strip off his clothes, and join me in the shower.

"Both are good." Soap spilling over my eyes, I stepped back under the spray to wash off. After getting dressed, I cleaned up the room and stuffed my dirty clothes into the gym bag. Dropping my bag by the front door, I caught a glimpse of Adam checking his hair in the microwave door.

"Feel better?" Carrying a bowl in one hand and a large dish in the other, he strolled out of the kitchen. "If you're off work and want a beer, you're welcome to grab one from the fridge. They're on the top shelf in the back so the kids can't reach them."

"Another glass of sweet tea like I had the other day would be good."

Adam nodded and sprinted back to the kitchen, bringing two glasses of tea when he returned. "I made salsa and queso since you like both."

Chips and queso was something I could eat my weight in. The way Adam made it was no exception. He'd mixed hamburger meat in with his goat cheese and added a few finely chopped peppers to spice it up.

"Are you the cook in the household?" Just as I voiced the question, he stuffed a chip in his mouth without breaking it. His mouth had stretched so wide to accommodate the entire chip that he couldn't speak. Covering his mouth with his hand, he tried to mumble an answer, but we both laughed at the attempt.

"Nod your head if yes," I suggested. Adam about choked on his bite after realizing how stupid it was to try and talk for a yes or no answer.

"I think Maggie loves me mostly for my cooking abilities. The smoke alarm is her timer." So, Maggie loved him. It could be a friendly type love. Then again, friendly love didn't explain three children. "Oh, I talked to her and she'd like to get the swing set built for next spring, if you're up for it."

"Absolutely. At the end of the season, I'll do my measurements and work it into my carpentry in the off season." For a few moments, we sat in silence. Only the sound of crunching chips could be heard.

Adam began flipping through channels on the television until he landed on something he liked. "Have you seen this?" On the screen was Emma Watson with very short hair. "It's *Perks of Being a Wallflower*. One of the few movies I enjoy more than the book." During the movie, I risked stolen glances at Adam, watching him fidget with a string on his shirt and occasionally cutting his eyes over toward me. I wondered if he wanted to kiss me right now half as much as I wanted to kiss him. It seemed doubtful.

The movie was mostly depressing with a few humorous moments thrown in. By the time the credits rolled, my face was damp due to the tears I tried to hold back but finally gave in to.

"Thanks for the happy entertainment this afternoon." Wiping his eyes, Adam chuckled. "It's a shitstorm of a life for the poor kid in that movie, but I can't help it. I love it so much."

"I can see why. I'm going to have to buy that one."

Mostly I wanted to watch it again to remember my day with Adam. I'd be curious to know if he thought of me next time he watched it.

Arms in the air, his elbows popping as he stretched, Adam gave a wide yawn. "Sorry, man. My body hasn't figured out I took the day off, so it's signaling me for bedtime."

"As long as you're not bored."

"Somehow I can't imagine you ever boring me." His tone was definitely flirtatious.

Standing to leave, I turned back. "Maybe you can cook for me again sometime." Two could play the flirting game.

"I'd be happy to."

Leaving Adam's house without getting to taste his succulent lips was not how I wanted the afternoon to end.

CHAPTER 6
ADAM

"Please tell me you aren't ogling the gardener again," Maggie groaned into the phone. She'd been rattling on for the past ten minutes about something at work, and I'd been ignoring her. It was hard to notice anything other than the tanned beauty outside. I'd already made excuses to talk to him by taking him water, then lemonade, and I asked him to join me for lunch. The last time we'd spent time together, he'd suggested I cook for him again, so today seemed as good a day as any.

"He's going to eat lunch with me today. I need to know which way this man swings because I'm looking to make a home run with him." I was ready to make my move.

"You're such a perv, Adam." Maggie laughed, not because it wasn't true but because she didn't think it was a bad thing. We'd become best friends the day we discovered we both had the dirtiest minds on the planet. A simple phrase could be twisted into something so dirty it was unsafe for television. Since fifth grade we'd been inseparable. In high school, we both fell for the same guy, but she won, given the fact he was straight and Maggie had the right parts. Donovan Summers had been a drummer in band—not in a band, but *the* band, as in marching band.

Band geeks were given a bad rap, but Donovan Summers was as cool as Steven Tyler himself. Golden locks of silky hair, soft hazel eyes with the power to melt hearts, and deep dimples attached to a gleaming smile sure to knock you off your feet. It wasn't hard to see how Maggie and I fell in love with him. Finding out he was straight broke my heart, but he and Maggie were perfect together. Instead of holding a grudge or letting it tear us apart, we embraced a friendship as the three musketeers.

No one had captured my eye since Donovan, no one who mattered. Until now. Eden, the gardener of all people. Nothing wrong with being a gardener; it just seemed a little clichéd, like falling for the handyman or the pool boy.

"If you don't ask him out over lunch, I'm going to have to address the situation myself." Maggie's threats were minimal but sincere. I'd been bending her ear about him since the first day he showed up on our doorstep.

"Don't worry, I'll undress him. I mean address them. Freudian slip?"

Maggie snorted loudly. "Sure it was. Go get him, boy."

I barked into the phone, then gave a few pants and whines before hanging up. As I turned around, I saw Eden standing in the doorway with a confused expression on his face. "Oh, sorry." Pointing at the phone, I said, "Maggie," as if that explained why I was barking like a dog. Eden nodded as if it were a completely normal response. The guy got my crazy—that was a plus.

CHAPTER 7
EDEN

THROUGH THE WINDOW I'D CAUGHT SIGHT OF ADAM squeezing the lemons for the delicious lemonade he kept bringing out to me. Afterward, I watched as he sucked lemon off his finger and made a sour face; it was sexy and hilarious at the same time. From outside, it appeared he and Maggie were married, but there were no pictures of them together in the house, which was odd to me. If I could get up the nerve to ask him, it would be much easier than all this wondering.

"Chicken?" Adam asked as I stood in the kitchen doorway staring at him.

"Excuse me?" *Can he read my mind and tell I'm struggling with nerves?*

"Do you eat chicken?"

"Yeah, of course. Can I help?" On the counter sat a

package of fresh chicken breasts, and next to it was a plate with flour and a bowl with an egg mixture.

"I hope you're a breast man," Adam teased. "While I fry up the chicken, you could chop up the potatoes and make some fries. Amber is napping, but she'll need food too when she wakes up. She loves french fries."

"So you have three kids?" Adam's head swung around, his eyebrows scrunched in confusion. "I saw the pictures. There's always three kids, but I've only met the shrieking wonder."

Loud laughter erupted from Adam. "The shrieking wonder, I love it! I may steal it. I usually call her little stink. But yes, there are three kids. One boy, two girl." Noticing I'd been searching the kitchen for the knives, he directed me to where I could find them. "Second drawer to the left. Under the sink there's a row of cutting boards, all sizes. Potatoes are in the bin next to the pantry."

"How old are your other kids?" I tried to make small talk as I made my way around the kitchen, following each of his directions. And I hoped to work in the "Are you married or do you find me sexy" question.

"Maggie's kids are four, six, and eight." His emphasis of Maggie's name was not lost on me. *If they aren't his kids, then how does he fit into this picture?*

"Oh. You're not their father?" Adam's eyes closed, his mouth falling into a frown. "None of my business, it was rude of me to ask. I apologize."

"It's fine. No, I'm not their father. He was my best friend, and he died a little more than a year ago from a brain tumor. They made me the godfather to all of their children, and they all call me Uncle Adam."

I felt like a tool for prying into what sounded like a very painful memory. A change of subject was needed. From what I'd witnessed of him with Maggie, I guessed they grieved together, which led to falling in love.

"Do you always feed the help?" Cutting up potatoes in a kitchen that wasn't mine started to make me feel weirder than the awkward conversation. A better subject didn't spring to mind quickly enough. Possibly one of the reasons I didn't date much was that I wasn't the greatest conversationalist.

Adam gave a hearty laugh that awakened the desire I'd been desperate to keep under wraps since I walked into the house. "You're not my butler or something. We've gotten to know each other a little. I'd like to call us friends. Is it weird?"

"I think friends is a good start." No one else had tried to get to know me like Adam. Clients treated me with kindness; sometimes the men talked about sports with me or the women would flirt or ask for gardening advice for in-between visits. But it was always short-lived and impersonal. Adam asked about me and what I wanted.

"Tell me about you. Married? Kids?"

"Neither. Hopefully one day. My niece is five. She's enough kid for me right now. My sister's marriage failed before it began, but not until she became pregnant. Before the divorce, she let him know about the baby in case it made him stay. His excuse was that he isn't the fatherly type. With him out of the picture, I stepped up to help her."

"Older or younger sister?" Adam didn't miss a beat in battering the chicken as he asked. He was quite the multitasker.

"Two years older. She's the only sibling I have. Do you have any siblings?" It was only fair for me to ask him a few questions as well.

"Nope. My parents got it right the first time and stopped with one." He grinned as I caught the semi-compliment in his comment, implying I was the right one that made them stop. It wasn't true in my family. My parents wanted to have a slew of children, but my mother lost two babies after me before giving up.

"So, why the name Eden? It's unusual?"

Rolling my eyes, I released an exaggerated breath. "Eden James. My parents are religious, very bible focused. Biblical names were bestowed upon us both, with hers being Eve Sara."

"Seems weird you were both named for two things associated with original sin," Adam commented.

"My parents went by the meanings of the names as well. For Eve, she was born on Christmas Eve so it had double meaning. Eden, though the garden associated with original sin, means delight. My mother loved the idea of the two E names for us and chose to ignore any negativity associated."

Adam nodded. "That explains the name of your company." Giving me a grin, he stuck his hands under the water to rinse the chicken off.

"The name Eden got me beat up a few times, so once I started high school I started going by my initials, EJ. Eve helped me come up with a name for my company, and I caved when she suggested using my first name. I don't mind the name so much anymore, plus it did seem incredibly appropriate for the type of business. And if I do say so myself, my yards do tend to have a godly beauty once I finish with them." It wasn't egotistical to be proud of your work, in my opinion.

"I'd have to agree. Your work is awe-inspiring. So, Eden? Can I call you Edie?" His eyebrows waggled teasingly.

"Do you enjoy your balls? Or would you like them

relocated?" To strengthen my threat, I held up the knife I'd been using on the potatoes.

Another hearty laugh exploded from Adam. Then in a low growl he replied, "I'm rather attached to the current placement of my balls." His gesture toward his crotch made my eyes drift down to his pants.

Desperate to hide my growing problem, I moved too close to the counter and the knife slipped in my hand and sliced open my palm. "Shit." The shrieking wonder walked in right at that exact moment and gave her banshee yell of distress, pushing Adam into action.

"Little stink, calm yourself." Her index finger shaking in my direction caught Adam's attention and he repeated my curse. "Shit." The banshee scream started once more. "Good grief, kid, we need to find a good use for those lungs. I'm going to rent you out for horror movies."

Nodding toward the back hallway, he said, "Down the hall, second door on your left is a bathroom with a first aid kit in the cabinet. It may need stitches. I'll come look at it once I get her settled for a movie." Scooping the child up in his arms, he ran out of the room with her, screams growing distant as he rounded the corner out of sight.

I made my way to the bathroom and found the first aid kit. There was blood on my pants, so I stripped them off to clean once I'd bandaged the cut. His order to wash the wound and let him check the boo-boo must be his paternal instinct at work. Maybe he'd kiss it and make it better. Perhaps I could find a few more boo-boos for him to kiss. *Dammit, Eden, get it together. He's possibly married and straight.*

Adam opened the door and jumped back. "Whoa, sorry, man. I thought it was your hand."

"It is, what's wrong?" His eyes lingered on me, and the room started to heat up.

"You took your pants off?" The corners of his mouth turned up in an odd grin.

"I got blood on them. I was about to run them under the water. I didn't think you'd be in here so quickly." My short gray boxer briefs felt practically invisible. And it was in that moment I realized my problem from earlier had returned, saluting Adam. His gaze was fixed on it, making my dick twitch with delight at the attention.

When he licked his lips, I almost came in my pants. Maybe he had an adventurous side? *Never mind, he's still married.* I'd never been one to break up a family.

If he doesn't quit ogling me, I won't be responsible for my actions.

"Can you help me with this?" I was referring to my hand, but honestly wanting help with… other things. I tried to hide my enjoyment at having Adam's gaze on me, but my cock had different ideas and wasn't going to sit down, instead straining to bust free of my boxer briefs.

Adam's voice cracked. "Excuse me?" His eyes were still glued to my crotch. Maybe he read my mind on what I really wanted—him down on his knees in front of me with eyes rolled up to meet mine as I disappeared into his mouth.

"My hand. Can you help me bandage it?"

"Oh yeah, sure." Taking my hand in his, he inspected the wound carefully. "No stitches needed. It bled quite a bit, but it's pretty superficial. Keep it clean, change the bandages, and put some Neosporin on it for a few days, and you'll be fine."

"Is that your expert dad opinion?"

"What?" Confusion colored his features and then a smile appeared. "Oh no. I work the night shift at the emergency room. I'm a trauma doctor."

He can play doctor with me anytime he wants to. I'd love to play with his stethoscope. Can I get a hot beef injection, stat? Code Blue Balls. A slew of other dirty doctor lines scurried through my mind. Spewing forth from my mouth were words of a less witty nature, lingering on the side of dorky. "Oh cool, I love *Grey's Anatomy.*" *Really, Eden, that's your response?*

Adam seemed to find it amusing, thankfully.

"Do you think I'm a Mark Sloan or Derek Shepherd?" Lifting his arm, he leaned his elbow against the door, crossing one leg over the other and giving me a sexy half smile.

"Shepherd for sure. Total McDreamy." *Shut up, Eden.* Beating myself up seemed silly over a little harmless flirting. "Look, I'll just come out and say it. You're a beautiful specimen of a man. If it makes you uncomfortable for me to say that, I'm sorry. I—"

My rant was cut short when Adam grabbed my face and pulled me forward for a kiss. A spine-tingling, toe-numbing, tongues-dancing-the-mamba kiss. I felt his reaction against my leg, and I wanted more. More of his mouth, more of his body against mine, more of our skin touching. That kiss was what I'd been yearning for. He tasted even better than I could have imagined. Grinding my hips against his, I dug my nails into his sides as my tongue explored the minty flavor of his mouth. Peppermint had just become my favorite flavor.

Caution thrown to the wind, I pushed my hands under his shirt, feeling his deliciously toned abs as his hands moved down to my ass, barely covered by my boxer briefs. Cupping my ass cheeks, he massaged as I thrust my hips into his.

Moving his hand around my waist, he slipped it over my erection and started to rub. I bucked against his hand, aching for the skin-to-skin sensation of his fingers wrapped around my length. He tugged at my briefs, releasing me, and when his hand grazed the tip, I almost came all over his palm.

Someone calling out from the other room broke the moment. Casually glancing at the door, Adam mumbled, "Damn, Mags is home for lunch."

I jerked my shorts up, moving to instant panic mode. *What have I done?*

"What?" I yelled, feeling totally fucked and not in the good way. Grabbing up the rest of my clothes, I quickly dressed as Adam stepped out of the room. He seemed so casual. If he wasn't freaked out about his wife coming home, why was I? They may have had an open marriage, for all I knew. It was possible she knew he was into men, possibly bisexual, and they'd worked out a deal.

Once I was ready, I bolted through the kitchen to the back door and yelled, "Thanks for bandaging my hand. I have to go."

Adam tried to have me stay, even Maggie called out to me, but I had overstayed my welcome. Only a few moments ago, I was about to have sex with a married man who was obviously confused about his sexuality, even if it didn't appear it was his first time touching a cock.

Damn, it had felt so amazing.

CHAPTER 8
ADAM

"WHAT DID I MISS?" MAGGIE ASKED, WIGGLING HER eyebrows.

"If you hadn't come home and ruined it, I would've gotten laid." Eden and I had been seconds away from afternoon delight on the bathroom counter. I'd have bent him over the sink and taken him if Maggie hadn't shown up. His growing excitement as I'd kissed him, running my hands over his smooth skin, the moans of desire he whimpered as I stroked him… it had all been so intensely passionate.

"You were going to do it with him with my child in the other room? Are you crazy?" Maggie smacked my arm, then sternly shook her finger at me.

"Doesn't matter, she was watching *Frozen*. For the next hour and a half, I could've torn the house down and rebuilt it around her and she'd never have noticed.

Do you know how long it's been since I've slept with a man?" Of course, I had been so lost in the moment I hadn't considered what would have happened if Amber had come out of her Disney stupor and come looking for me. I wasn't even sure I had the bathroom door locked.

"So why did he run out of here so quickly?"

"I have no idea! We were doing great until he heard your voice. Maybe he's not out of the closet yet? At first he definitely seemed surprised when I kissed him." His surprise had been short-lived as he gave in to the kiss, matching my tongue movements, his moans driving me to push us to the next step so quickly and begin to remove his clothes.

"Maybe he's not gay?"

"Oh no, there's no doubt he was into me." Before I'd walked into the room I'd had doubts, but when I saw him standing there in nothing but his underwear, sporting wood, I'd known he'd been feeling the same things I had.

"Wonder what spooked him?" Maggie and I exchanged a glance and a shrug. "Guess you can ask him when he comes back in two weeks. Or you could text him and ask what happened." Checking her phone, she mumbled a curse as she read the text about an issue at her job needing immediate attention. "I need to get back to work. I'll just grab a protein shake from the fridge. Damn, chicken and fries a la Adam sounded delish."

"I'll save you some for dinner." She kissed me on the lips. We always kissed on cheeks or lips, but right then I wished she hadn't kissed me there. I wanted the taste of Eden to linger for a bit.

"You're the best, Adam. I couldn't do any of this without you. I know the kids and I have put a damper on your love life since you moved in, but it's going to get better."

It had put a damper on my dating, but I wouldn't have had it any other way. Deserting my best friend in her time of grief in order to get laid would be the most selfish act.

"Mags, you and these kids are my life. I loved Donovan too, and being here has helped me heal. Besides, I still have many years of hotness ahead for me." I winked, and she pulled me into a hug before grabbing a protein shake from the fridge and running out the door.

Opening my laptop, I stared at Eden's picture on the screen as his page was still pulled up on my Facebook app. I must have been staring for a while, lost in lusty thoughts, when a small voice from the living room pulled me from my musings. "Uncle Adam?" *Frozen* had ended and the shrieking wonder was awake. Screaming at the top of her lungs was a trait taught to her by her father. In trying to teach her about stranger danger, they'd told her if she were ever scared or needed help to scream as loud as possible and Donovan promised he'd come running. Now we couldn't break her of the habit. Once in a while, she shrieked in the middle of the night, each time for the same reason: she woke up missing her dad and shrieked hoping to bring him running.

"Hey, little stink. We've been stuck in this house for too long today. What would you say if we took a trip to the zoo?" Distraction was my goal. Sitting in the house for the rest of the day would certainly lead to dreaming of Eden.

Bright blue eyes widened as a smile of pure joy filled her face. "Yes!"

"Do me a favor, no shrieking at the zoo. Remember, it makes the animals more scared than you." It happened once before at a pet store. Something spooked Amber and every animal in the store went wild, banging against cages, howling, even hissing. The manager rightfully asked us never to return. Maggie had never wanted to get the kids a dog that day as it was, so she was pretty happy with the result.

"Okay. You'll hold my hand the whole time?"

Kissing her forehead, I lifted her up onto my hip and carried her upstairs to get into some new clothes. Anytime we stayed at home she insisted on wearing pajamas. There were times she wanted to wear pajamas to the grocery store. Breaking this girl of habits was an impossible feat.

———

Taking Amber to the zoo hadn't been the best idea. Luckily there wasn't a shrieking event; however, we did get close to one at the petting zoo portion. A llama strutted over and I snatched Amber up and ran her out of there before she shrieked and made it spit on us. At the tiger exhibit, she convinced me to wait around until one of them appeared. They'd been in the back of the cage sleeping—until the dinner bell rang.

We were there so long I barely got home in time for a nap before work. Maggie woke me when she realized I had slept through my alarm. I had fifteen minutes to get ready and go. Spritzing on a little cologne and jumping into my scrubs, I prayed for a slow night so I'd have time for a shower at some point.

No such luck.

As soon as I walked in the door, I was grabbed by a nurse. "We have two ambulances on their way, a four-car pileup on the highway. Two critical, two with minor injuries." Shoving a chart at me, she added, "You also have a broken ankle in room three, a toddler with a high fever in two, and a man with severe abdominal pains in room one."

"Critical by ambulance? Where's life flight?" Critical cases came in by helicopter to avoid the time lapse getting to the hospital due to traffic. "And am I the only damn doctor here tonight?" One or two cases I could handle, but I'd have to prioritize the five patients thrown at me. A broken bone could wait longer than severe abdominal pains or a high fever. They drew the short end of the stick, earning the longest wait time.

"They were working another wreck already, no more room. The victims of that crash are en route as we speak to Stonecrest because it's closer. Dr. Jennings is on call. I've paged him and he'll be in within the hour. If you need a specialist, I'll page them the minute you tell me." Stonecrest Hospital was in a town outside Nashville, and had a helipad out front of their emergency room. Ours was on the roof, which made it a little less convenient, but we're in downtown Nashville.

"Give me five minutes to scrub up, and I'll be ready when they get here."

"Make it four, Adam. One is a child." No need to be told twice, I sprinted down the hallway to the scrub room. Running scalding hot water over my hands, I soaped them up, scrubbing almost to my elbows before rinsing off. Shaking my hands dry, I turned to the scrub nurse, who applied gloves for me.

Every patient, no matter the age, was important, but children always grabbed our attention the quickest. Rushing through the doors of the trauma entrance, I spotted the paramedics working on the little girl. She was so tiny, she couldn't be much older than Amber. Fragile and pale, one hand hung down off the stretcher limply.

"Fill me in," I said to the paramedics as I started looking the girl over for injuries, holding her wrist to check her heart rate. It was faint, but it was there. *Thank goodness.* Grabbing a penlight from my pocket, I lifted her eyelids one at a time to check her pupil response.

"She was in the back seat. Restrained in her car seat, but the impact was so strong the buckle broke, sending her face-first into the back of the driver seat. Her mother was driving, she's behind us in the other ambulance. According to her, the girl stopped speaking shortly after impact. We have a pulse, but she hasn't regained consciousness yet. From a glance it appears she has a broken arm, possibly a broken rib as well. It's hard to tell without her letting us know what hurts."

"Take her into trauma one," I requested of the paramedic before turning to a nurse. "Page pediatrics, stat." Doors burst open again with the mother, whose clothes were covered in blood. Her tibia had broken through the skin and her neck was braced. Blood never made me queasy, but seeing bones breaking through the skin was enough to make anyone's stomach roll.

Pulling me aside, the medic stated, "She was cut from the car and screaming about her child. Obviously her leg is broken. She's lost a lot of blood and she passed out shortly after we removed her." Poor woman would wake up in a lot of pain, worried sick about her daughter. She didn't have a fun night ahead of her.

Next to me the nurse took notes as I rattled off information. "We need a full run of tests on her to check for internal bleeding. Page an orthopedic surgeon to set that break. I'll watch for her test results and see if I need to take her to surgery. Give her information to Luann, at the desk, and find next of kin, maybe the father for the child?" Nights like this one made me hate my job. We could potentially lose a mother and daughter, or have to tell one or the other that the most important person in their life was gone. If we were lucky, both of them would pull through with flying colors.

While awaiting results, I checked on the charts of some of the other patients in the waiting room to see who I could take care of and send on their way quicker. Just a glance at the mother and daughter told me they'd both need surgery of some kind. If the mother was blessed, she'd only need an open reduction of her fractured bone. The little girl… I was afraid that with her unconscious state she may not be as fortunate.

Walking to the nurse's desk, I heard someone ask, "Is this Eden Coleman? Are you related to Eve Coleman? Sir, she's been in an accident. Are you the child's father? Oh, okay. Do you know who the father is? We have you listed as Eve's next of kin, but nothing for the child. I understand… Yes, they just arrived so I have no other news for you."

It couldn't be possible there were two sets of people named Eden and Eve, right? How many guys had that name anyway? My heart began to race with worry as to Eden's mental state over hearing that his sister and niece were injured. Dropping the chart in my hand, I sprinted off to check on Eve.

"Can I get an update, please?"

"I'll bring it to you when she's done," the tech snapped impatiently. We doctors dealt with that occasionally. Most techs assumed we thought we were better than them, though I didn't think I treated them that way—or at least I never meant to.

"She's the sister of a friend. I want to brace him for what's coming."

Sighing in annoyance, he caved and gave me the information I needed. "Based on what I've seen so far, she has a few cracked ribs. An open fracture of the tibia, a nondisplaced fracture of the femur, and a pretty sizeable head contusion. With a few surgeries, and a long recovery, she should be fine."

"Thanks, man, I appreciate the help." Now I needed to find out about her daughter's prognosis. Per the nurse, her name was Jacqueline, and pediatrics had taken her into surgery immediately due to bleeding on her brain. She'd been unconscious for a while, which meant things weren't looking as hopeful. Commotion down the hall caught my attention.

"Dammit, I don't know what the code is! I'm her brother and I need to know she's okay. Can you please help me? I don't give a flying fuck about privacy matters!" Eden's hands slammed down on the counter, making the nurse jump back in fear.

I placed my hand on Eden's shoulder, then jerked back when he swung around with his fist up. Surprise replaced the anger. "Adam?" Once realization hit, he wrapped his arms around me in relief. "Please help me find my sister," he whispered against my ear, gripping me so tightly I could hardly breathe.

Rubbing his back, I tried to calm him. "Katie, I'm going to walk to a private room to speak with my friend here." I wanted the nurse to be aware of his location in case there was news about his family.

With the grip he had on me, I didn't want to stray far from him. I grabbed his hand and led him to the private room we used to speak with family members. Closing the door, I stepped over to the water cooler, pulled out a cup, and filled it for him. I scooted my chair up next to him and took his hands in mine. "I saw Eve when she came in. I didn't know who she was, but I sent her for tests. When I overheard the nurse talking to you on the phone, I made sure to get as much detail as I could. It's going to sound bad, and I want you to know she's going to be in pain and it's going to be a long recovery, but in the long run she'll be back to herself one day." Explaining each injury made his face scrunch in pain more until he let himself release the emotions. Watching the tears pour down his face shattered my heart.

Again, I pulled him close for a hug, running my hands through his hair. "There's more." I gently rubbed his back. I needed to quiet him so he could take in the news about his niece.

Being a trauma doctor, giving bad news was a pretty common event. Most days I could be numb to the emotions, but today was not one of those days. Eden's sobs touched a place no one but Donovan and Maggie had ever touched. A man I barely knew held my heart in his hands. "Jacqueline is your niece, right?"

"Jackie." Her name escaped his mouth in a whisper of emotions as he nodded.

I stroked his cheek with my thumb, then placed my palm at the back of his head. "The impact of the crash broke the seat belt holding in her car seat. Being confined protected most of her bones, but she hit her head pretty hard. There was some swelling on her brain and she needed surgery." News of her injuries almost broke him completely. If I could have stayed with him all night, I would have without thinking twice, but my pager went off, drawing me back to reality. "I have to go, Eden. If you need anything, you have me paged. When my shift is over, I'll sit with you."

Stepping out of the room, I took a deep breath to regain my composure and headed back to the desk for my next assignment. A local sheriff had been brought in for stomach pain and had been diagnosed with appendicitis while I'd been tending to Eden. For the next hour or so, I'd be performing an emergency appendectomy.

Scrubbing in for the surgery, I ran the water for much longer than needed. My surgical assistant waved her hand in front of my face, bringing me back to reality. In order to be sure the surgery was successful, I had to push Eden out of my mind.

It was the most difficult hour of my life.

CHAPTER 9
EDEN

If Adam hadn't been the one to tell me the news, I don't know if I could have handled it. Now that he'd seen me sobbing like a crazy person, it most likely killed any attraction he had for me. My sister and I had been through too much together. Losing her, or my niece, would be the death of me. Deep down I knew Adam had to work, but I ached for him to be near me. With him holding my hand, I would have the strength and patience to push forward. He'd been so kind in sitting with me and putting their injuries into terms I understood.

A sign on the wall caught my eye. Chapel was written with an arrow pointing down the hallway to the right. Following the arrow, I found the small sanc-tuary and stepped inside. A row of five or six pews on either side with an aisle in between led up to a crucifix with a kneeling rail in front. Genuflecting in front of the cross, I hoped I wasn't struck down for being in a church after so many years. Whenever anyone was sick, my parents would light a candle and say a prayer. Faith had never been an easy thing for me. Prayer was certainly not something I did often, if ever. Growing up in a Catholic family, I recited the prayers and followed all the motions, but never felt it meant anything.

Striking a match, I lit a candle for Eve and one for Jackie. Dropping to my knees, I placed my hands together and bowed my head. "Not sure how to word this. I'm used to reciting the words without thinking. All I know is I want my sister and niece to be happy and well. If I can do anything to make this happen.... I'll make any sacrifice I have to in order to keep them around. I need a sign."

And at that very moment, someone walked up behind me and placed a hand on my shoulder. "Eden?" Maggie stood smiling down at me. "I brought Adam his lunch. He ran out of the house in a hurry this evening. I asked my neighbor to sit with the kids while I ran over here." Glancing around, she checked for signs of others in the room, and lowered her voice. "He told me about your sister and niece. Technically, he isn't supposed to, so please don't be angry with him. He asked me to check in on you. He's quite worried. Is there anything I can do?"

Last time I saw Maggie was when I ran out the door of her house after almost having sex with her male housemate and possibly partner. Was that why I was sitting there grieving right now? Were my actions responsible for my family being in pain? I'd broken a commandment. I was raised to believe breaking those came with consequences. Gazing up at the crucifix on the wall, I mumbled an almost inaudible, "Please forgive me for my sins. Do not punish my family." Deep down I knew these thoughts were ridiculous, but my emotions ran the gauntlet when Eve or Jackie were involved.

"I shouldn't have bothered you while you're praying. I'm so sorry." Maggie turned toward the exit, but I grabbed her hand. "Do you want me to stay?" I nodded, but was unsure why I wanted her to stay and stoke my guilt more.

"It's very kind of you to stop to see me. I'm not a person who prays, but it seemed like a good time to start. My parents used to scold me and say I needed to pray even when I didn't want something, but I never knew what to say. If there's nothing I want, what's there to pray about?" Logic had played a major part in my lack of faith over the years.

"I was raised Catholic myself. Most of prayer is meant to be for giving thanks." Maggie turned toward the crucifix at the front of the chapel and took my hand. "We'd like to give thanks to you for bringing Eden's family to the ER where they can receive the best help possible. As grateful as we are, we have one more request, please protect…." Turning her gaze to me, she waited for the names of my sister and niece.

"Eve and Jackie," I added.

"Please protect Eve and Jackie and the doctors who are caring for them now. Amen." Shrugging, she said to me, "I've never been good at praying either, but I figure if you word it just right, she'll get the idea."

"She?"

"Oh please, everyone knows God's really a woman." Maggie winked and bumped shoulders with me, making me laugh for the first time in, what felt like, hours.

"I'm sorry about earlier."

Forehead scrunched, Maggie's eyes lowered. "Earlier?"

"When I ran out of the house. I was late for another job." A lie told in a church has to be a greater sin than any other lie, but I needed to apologize, and what else could I say about why I left?

Other than "I'm a big home-wrecking tramp."

"It's no problem. Adam was a bit disappointed though. He loves having people try his famous fried chicken." Either this woman had no clue about Adam, or she was the best actress ever. Eyes lighting up with a sudden thought, she grabbed my arm gently. "Come to dinner."

"There's no way I can leave my family right now."

"Of course not. I'm sorry, not tonight." She glanced at her watch and corrected herself, "Sorry, tomorrow. When they're home, we'll schedule an evening for you to come over. In fact, you could bring them as well, if you'd like to."

Any future plans, especially involving Maggie or Adam, seemed pointless to make at that moment. The more time I spent standing next to her, the more the guilt inside ate away at me. "I need to get back to check on my sister and niece. Thanks for stopping by to check on me. I'll give you a call about the rest of the summer. I may need to refer you to another landscaper for the last few weeks."

Life as I knew it would change dramatically until Eve was better. My landscaping business became a carpentry business in the fall and winter months. Building furniture, working on houses, anything I could do with my hands. It may become my only source of income for a while until she was back to her old self.

"I understand. Definitely give me a call. I appreciate the amazing job you've done. And you've been so kind to my family. I feel like we've developed a bit of a friendship. I hope you feel the same." Nothing about this woman was fake; it was easy to see what made Adam love her.

All I could muster was a polite smile and a nod. Opening the door of the chapel, I extended my hand for her to go first and was grateful to see her move in the opposite direction of me. I hurried down the hallway to get an update. Adam was standing at the nurses' station. Before I had time to turn and run, our eyes met and his lips turned up in a smile, lighting up his face. Could he return my feelings? It didn't matter; my top priority was my family.

CHAPTER 10
ADAM

After my shift was over, I went to check on Eve and Jackie before I left. Checking the computer for the room number, I was glad to see Eve was in a private room, not the ICU. Since she didn't know me, I went in under the guise of checking in on her. "Ms. Coleman?" I asked as I knocked on the door. "I'm Dr. Simmons. I saw you when you were first brought in." Most of her lower body was in a cast, and from the lump under her gown, I knew her ribs were wrapped tightly. Her eyes matched Eden's, hazel specks with a pale green iris. I could see the same kindness behind them.

"My daughter," she whispered. "Is my daughter awake yet?" When her face had hit the air bag, it had torn her lip open. The stitches and swelling made it difficult for her to speak loudly.

"I can find out." As simple as the request was, I didn't know how good the news would be or how well she could handle bad news.

"My brother went to check on her, but he hasn't been back. I'm very worried."

"Let me see if I can find your brother and daughter. I'll be back in a moment." The door opened and Eden stepped into the room, mouth opening in surprise when he spotted me.

"I'm back, Eve. Jackie is out of surgery and in recovery. Doctor says everything went well and she's going to be fine." After assuring his sister, he whispered to me, "What are you doing here?"

"Checking on Eve… and you. Can we talk outside? My shift is over, maybe I can buy you breakfast?" My shift had been long and exhausting, but right then I wanted to be next to Eden more than anything else. Based on his sullen expression, he needed a friend to lean on.

"Go with him, Eden. I'm fine. Now that I know my daughter is safe, I can sleep."

"I'll be back before you know I'm gone." Eve tried to smile, but it came out more as a grimace. Kissing her forehead, he whispered, "I love you," before following me out the door.

Picking up a few biscuits at a fast-food restaurant

down the street, we sat in my car to talk. I offered to take him to a restaurant, but he refused, saying he didn't want to be around all those people right then. Being alone with him was better for me, too. Only the sound of chewing and paper crackling filled the car for a few awkward moments. Watching his mouth move as he ate, his tongue darting out to catch crumbs, made me miss his mouth. We'd shared one incredible kiss, and I couldn't get it out of my mind.

"Thanks for everything tonight."

"I didn't do much." Two other doctors had performed the surgeries on Eve and Jackie, so I couldn't take credit for any healing.

"You did more than you know. Having a shoulder to lean on meant more than anything. Eve and Jackie are my life. Tonight I thought I could lose them, and the only thing keeping me from falling into a pit of despair was you."

"They're both going to be fine. I wouldn't lie to you. I've seen how sugarcoating the truth prolongs the pain."

"With Maggie and her last husband?" Eden peered up at me curiously.

"Two years ago, Donovan was diagnosed with a malignant brain tumor. The doctors gave him three months. In the beginning, he didn't want Maggie to know how short of a time he had. He didn't think she could handle it. He fought as hard as he could, desperate for as much time with his kids and Maggie as he could muster. Eventually he lost the battle, but not until he'd lived another eight months past expectations." Tears fell from my eyes; I didn't even try to hold them back. With Eden, I felt no need to hide who I was or what I was feeling.

"How long did he hide the truth from her?"

"For three months. She was angry, but didn't hold on to the anger because she needed every minute with him." Maggie and I kept smiles on for the kids, but there were times we sent them to their grandparents for the weekend so we could share memories, drink wine, and shed a few tears over our lost love. Even in the end, when I saw how much he loved Maggie, he always held a special place in my heart.

"You loved him almost as much as she did, didn't you?"

Eden leaned over to touch my hand, and I took advantage of the moment to capture his lips with mine. At first he pulled away in shock. Placing my palm against his cheek, I gazed into those beautiful green eyes and pulled him forward once more, taking his lower lip between mine and sucking on it lightly before moving to the top lip. I slid my tongue between his lips, and my cock jerked when he moaned against my mouth.

Moving my mouth across his jaw, I tasted my way to his ear, where I began to suck on the lobe. "I've wanted you since you first showed up at my house. I can't stop thinking about you." Guiding my hand to his pants as I spoke, I felt his excitement grow. "Do you want me?"

Eden hesitated only briefly before biting his lip and nodding. "More than anything."

Unzipping his pants, I stroked him through his boxers. "Lay the seat back. Let me help you forget about everything for a few minutes." We were far away from any curious eyes, and it was still dark outside for at least another hour.

Tasting the precum at the tip of his engorged cock, I swirled my tongue around the outside before taking him as far into my throat as I could. Eden's hand grasped my hair, guiding me up and down to the rhythm of his moans. A salty-sweet taste filled my mouth as he bucked beneath me, calling out my name. I wanted to be home in my bed where I could lay him down on soft silk sheets and fill him to the brink, satisfy him for hours and show him just how much I wanted him.

Moving over top of him on the seat, I leaned down to taste his lips again. "Come home with me?" I whispered against his mouth. "Let me show you what else I can do." Something awakened in Eden's eyes; it looked like regret and it tore at my very soul. Backing away, I rolled back over to my seat. Now the only thing between us was silence.

Zipping up his pants, Eden never looked at me. "I'm sorry, Adam. I'm so sorry." And he got out of the car and walked out of my life.

The next day he called Maggie and referred her to a new landscaper. His excuse was that he'd be living with Eve and Jackie for a while and needed to focus on them. It seemed the real reason was whatever happened to spook him that day between us.

THE NEW LANDSCAPER COULDN'T HOLD A CANDLE TO Eden. He was an older gentleman who barely grunted a hello when he came over. His wife helped him prune bushes and she tended to the flowers while he mowed the grass. They did a good job, but they weren't very friendly. I missed Eden. More than only the passion between us, I missed the little chats we'd had. Calling Amber the shrieking wonder had become my thing lately. Each time I said it, my heart broke a little more, but I couldn't break the habit.

One day I stole Maggie's phone to call Eden, knowing he'd never answer my number.

"Maggie, how is the new landscaper working out?"

"Eden, can we please talk?" His professional demeanor changed drastically when he heard my voice on the line instead. Instantly, he turned cold.

"I'm busy, Adam. I have to go. I'm sorry."

I didn't know what I'd done to drive him away.

CHAPTER 11
EDEN

It'd been six months since the car accident. Eve and Jackie were back to normal, which meant my life could resume. During those six months, I'd had to sublet my apartment so I could move in with Eve full-time to help and save money in the process. Utilizing her large garage, I built furniture during the day and sometimes at night when I couldn't sleep. Sometimes it was the strange bed plus the surroundings; other times it was due to dreams of Adam.

A local store had requested a number of items from me for before Christmas. With it came a nice chunk of change, allowing me to take a month off in January to take Eve and Jackie to stay at a condo on the beach for a few days. All of us needed to get out of the house and away from town for a while. Being cooped up inside, barely going anywhere farther than the closest grocery store, had caused us to go a bit stir-crazy with cabin fever.

Sleeping had become a thing of the past for me. Each time I closed my eyes I could see Adam's face, feel his lips on mine, remember how it felt to be in his mouth. It had been the most erotic thing I'd ever experienced. When he'd asked me to come home with him, part of me wanted to shout, "Yes, please, now!" until I saw Maggie's face in my mind. Why didn't I ask him about their relationship? Instead of letting so much time pass without speaking to him, I should have called and talked it over. From everything I'd learned about Adam, I couldn't imagine him being the kind of man who would cheat on his wife. There must be more to the story, but it seemed too late to change things now.

Eve sensed early on that I was in heartbreak mode. When I told her who Adam was, the doctor, she wasn't ashamed of me, only disappointed that we couldn't be together. He'd called a few times, and I wanted to talk to him, but I couldn't. Hearing his voice stirred feelings inside I couldn't handle on my own. We hadn't known each other for long, but I knew I was in love because nothing other than love could be as painful as thinking of Adam.

It was springtime now, and I needed to get back to landscaping work. One name on my list had me dreading it, Maggie Summers. Eve held my clipboard. "I thought Adam's last name was Simmons?"

"I think so, why?" Truth be told, I hadn't asked his last name. Eve knew from when she'd met him in the hospital.

"So if he's married, why does she have a different name?" Tapping her finger against the clipboard, she raised her eyebrow in question.

"Don't ask me. Maybe it's because she was married before and wants to keep the same name as her kids? You changed your name back to Coleman when your douchebag husband left." It wasn't unusual for married couples to have different last names these days. Some women never changed theirs. I'd seen the name Summers written on some of the kids' stuff when I'd been in the house, so I assumed it was Donovan's last name.

"Or maybe you should verify they are in fact married. You've never asked him, have you?" Eve was smarter than me any day of the week. Like an idiot, it had never occurred to me to come right out and ask. Maybe I'd thought asking would confirm what I suspected and make the guilt worse. "When you see him today, ask. Bring it up casually somehow."

"What do you mean, like 'hey, thanks for that great blow job, did you learn the technique from your wife'?" Snatching the clipboard out of her hand, I shoved it into my backpack. Hand gripping the handle of the cooler, I dragged it behind me and slammed the door on my way out. Seeing Adam today would be awkward, but taking my anxiety out on Eve wasn't fair.

Outside Maggie's house, I sat in the van for thirty minutes, wishing Adam's car would disappear before I had to get to work. A tap on the window jerked me out of my daydream. Beautiful blue eyes and a scruffy, unshaven face that couldn't hide a gleaming white smile greeted me. He was every bit as beautiful as I remembered. Lost in his gaze, I almost forgot how to lower the pane of glass shielding me from his voice.

"How've you been?" Adam asked as soon as I remembered how to roll the window down. Crossing his arms on the windowsill, he leaned forward, dangerously close to me. The woodsy scent of his cologne invaded my nose. Between his smell and his tongue gliding across his lips to wet them, I was hard as a rock already.

"Good. Sorry, I had a little paperwork to do since I was running early. I'll get started. I have a new contract for your wife if she's home." I'd practiced saying wife all the way over. Shocked as I was to hear the word spill freely from my mouth, Adam seemed even more startled by the comment.

"Eden, we need to talk. No one's home right now.

Maggie took Amber to register for her first school year." He placed his hand on my shoulder, his eyes searching mine. "Please."

Avoiding eye contact, I lowered my gaze to my clipboard. "I have another house after this one. I should—"

"I'll make it fast, I promise." Adam opened the door for me. Reluctantly, I slid out of the car, pushing the lock button before shutting the door. Walking behind Adam, I couldn't stop myself from noticing how nice his ass looked in his jeans. Going into an empty house full of beds, couches, tables, and many other places to have sex, wasn't what I had in mind for today. Logic flew out the window anytime I was around Adam.

Nothing had changed since the last time I was here. Everything was in its place; still no pictures of the happy couple. Why wouldn't he go with her for Amber's registration? He may not have been her biological father, but he was at least her stepdad. "Sit, please," Adam insisted.

He sat down beside me, and I grew nervous at the proximity of our bodies. After all this time, he still affected me. "What did you want to talk about?"

"We shared something last summer. I want to know why you ran away. I think I might have finally figured it out. Is it because of what you said, Maggie is my wife?" Arm on the back of the couch, he leaned in closer.

"I don't want to come between a married couple. If you're unsure of your sexuality or wanting to explore other opportunities, that's up to you and your wife. For me, I can't be part of it. I have real feelings for you."

Laughter erupted from Adam, and it hurt. I couldn't believe I'd confessed my feelings for him and he'd responded with laughter. Perhaps I'd truly misjudged him.

"Maggie and I are not married. She's my best friend. I moved in with her after Donovan died. For two months, Maggie lay in her room refusing to leave, clinging to a pillow, wearing only clothes that had belonged to Donovan. Her kids were being ignored, the grief had consumed her. Bills had piled up from hospital visits and bucket list items they lived out together. Combining our paychecks was the only way to keep her head above water. I took on the night shift so I could take care of Amber." Sliding closer to me, he placed his hand on my knee. "Since puberty hit, I've known I was into guys and not gals. I was in love with someone in this house, but it was Donovan, not Maggie. They both knew about my feelings too, but it didn't change our friendship."

Knowing he wasn't married or involved lifted an unbearable weight from my shoulders. If only I'd asked about his relationship months ago, maybe we could've had something together. "Dammit."

"What?" Adam reached up and stroked my cheek.

Laying my head against his hand, I closed my eyes, relishing the feel of his skin against mine. "I've been incredibly stupid."

"We both were. Talking things out would have been the way to go."

"We could talk now. Get to know one another again." Checking my watch, I calculated the amount of time I'd need for the yard. "I have about an hour to spare today. I didn't expect we'd talk. I planned to speed through the yard and get out of here as quick as possible."

"I'm glad I stuck around. I've been worried you would tell Maggie you couldn't do her yard anymore." The thought had crossed my mind, but in the end I had to think about my business over my pride.

"You look good with the scruffy beard. I'm used to seeing you clean-shaven, but I like this look too." I traced my fingers across the stubble on his jaw, and Adam grinned widely.

"It's the graveyard-double-shift look. I've been working my ass off to avoid any free time...." He trailed off without explaining further. Sheepishly, he glanced away from me.

"What's wrong? Why didn't you want free time?"

For a moment, he kept his gaze focused across the room. Then it dawned on me. "Oh. Because of me?"

He nodded ever so slightly, his Adam's apple bobbing as he swallowed. "You're all I've thought about for months. Staying busy kept me sane. It sounds crazy, I know. We barely know each other, but you left an imprint on my life, Eden."

"I feel the same way about you. Although, I can say heartache is good for my carpentry business. You should see all the furniture I built in the last few months." Awkward laughter erupted from me. The sound was so foreign I crinkled my forehead, confused at my own reaction. "I truly am—" Before I could apologize again, Adam placed his finger against my lips.

"Right now, let's stop saying we're sorry. It was a misunderstanding, and it's time to move forward." Extending his hand out toward me, he added, "Deal?"

With a firm shake, I responded, "Deal."

Tracing his finger across my cheek, he asked, "Now to the question I've been wanting to ask since you got here. Are you seeing anyone?"

"No. No one since I met you." It wasn't as if I'd had any hope for a future with Adam and saved myself for him, but since the day I met him, I hadn't been able to get him off my mind. Like the first book in a cliffhanger series, he left me wanting more. Each night ended with a thought of him, each morning began the same.

Moving his hand away from my cheek, Adam reached for mine. "Would you go on a date with me?" He batted his eyelashes in a teasing fashion, and I admired his adorable face, unable to speak. Feeling like a teenager getting asked out by the coolest guy in school, complete with butterflies, clammy hands, and lack of speaking ability, I eventually managed to squeak out, "Yes."

"Tomorrow evening I'm off work. Can I pick you up at seven?" No time was wasted in making plans. No empty promises of "let's do lunch" without specific dates and times in place. We were scheduling a date.

"I'll pick you up. I know where you live." With a wink, I let go of his hand. "For now, I need to get to work."

CHAPTER 12
ADAM

MAGGIE WAS ECSTATIC TO HEAR ABOUT MY DATE PLANS with Eden. After laughing for quite a while about the thought of being married to me, she finally calmed long enough to give me some good advice. "Not many people get second chances like this, Adam. Don't take it for granted. Be honest with one another and you'll make it work. The way he looks at you, it's the way Donovan looked at me. There's a lot of love there."

"Slow down a little, Mags. It's our first official date, not a marriage proposal yet."

"Yet?" she questioned hopefully.

"It's not out of the question. I like Eden, a lot. It's rather possible I'm in love with him already. Even so, I want to do this right. We're taking things slow." The slower the better. Heartache was something I couldn't bear again right now. When Eden walked away from me a few months ago, I threw myself into work, taking on extra shifts, volunteering for special projects, and refused to spend a moment at home alone to live with my heartbreak.

Maggie laughed. "I'm not sure you know how to go slow. Am I mistaken or did you not gobble his knob in the parking lot of your work?"

"You're so trashy." Giving her a wink, I grabbed her up in a hug. "One of the things I love most about you."

Grabbing my cheeks, she grinned. "It's been a long time since I've seen such happiness in your eyes. I owe Eden a thank-you."

"We need to get the sparkle back in your eyes too. It's been almost two years since Donovan died. He'd want more for your life than just work and Netflix binging." Nights when I worked, Maggie spent time with the kids before sitting up most of the night watching her favorite shows on Netflix instead of sleeping. It had taken her a year to sleep in their bed again after Donovan died. One night I tricked her by getting her drunk and carrying her to the room to sleep. The next morning, I awoke to her screaming followed by glass breaking. By the time I got to her, she'd smashed every picture along with the large mirror on her closet. Blood trickled across her wrists from the cuts obtained while breaking things. At first glance, I thought she'd tried to commit suicide.

"Donovan was my one great love. I can't ask for more. My kids, and you, give me all the happiness I need." Her smile was so sincere, it couldn't be faked, but still I wanted more for her. Someone out there could love her the way Donovan had, the way she deserved to be loved.

"Not to be crude, but you need a man to come over and go downstairs for breakfast." Her blank expression showed she wasn't following the slang. "Kneel at the altar? Munch the bearded clam? Medicate the hairy papercut? Talk to the boat people?"

"I get it!" Shoving me playfully, she grunted in annoyance. "Who comes up with those crazy names for it? Hairy papercut?" Making a V with her hands, she motioned to her crotch and said, "This has never been hairy. Just FYI."

"Wrong abbreviation, that's TMI. I don't need to know what kind of haircut your monkey has." Too much information wasn't a thing between Maggie and me. We'd gone skinny-dipping together. I'd seen her naked almost as many times as I'd seen myself naked. I could appreciate a beautiful body, and I knew hers was phenomenal, but it'd never gotten my motor running.

"Seriously, Mags. You should date again. You're a beautiful, fun, sweet woman and there is someone out there worthy of you." Tears filled her eyes. When they fell, I wiped them away with my thumb.

"Flirting with someone feels like I'm cheating on Donovan. I'm not sure how I can date with such guilt on my conscience." She'd only been with one man in her life, so I could understand why she was nervous about being with someone else. And I'd seen Maggie flirt. It was like watching a baby bird try to fly for the first time, sort of cute but mostly awkward and sad.

"Just before he passed away, we had a talk about you. He knew you'd be a hard sell on dating again. He asked me to promise that when I thought you were ready, to let you know. I've been watching you work your ass off the last couple of years. You have the kids and they make you happy, but there is always this little bit of sadness still in your eyes."

Moving away from me, she cleared her throat, looking at the ceiling as she wiped the tears away. "Give me a little more time. Let's focus on you and Eden first. Let's get you ready for your date and talk about mine another day." She held her hand out for a shake, and I accepted her terms by grasping it.

"Please be cool when he gets here."

She wiggled her eyebrows, and I knew she had devious plans, the opposite of cool. And I was right. When the doorbell rang, she beat me to the door. Grabbing his arm, she pulled him inside. "Where are you taking him?" she demanded. Anxious to finish getting ready before he saw me, I stayed out of sight and listened to them.

"Well, he asked me out, so it's up to him." Hearing the nerves in Eden's voice made me grin. Even after being intimate with each other, he still got nervous around me, and it was adorable. I'd make sure to make him as comfortable as possible because I had a lot of hot moments in mind for him.

"I'm thrilled you two are going out. I have to admit, you gave me a great laugh when Adam told me you thought we were married." She placed her hand on Eden's arm, and they both had another laugh. Eden's laughter had a nervous edge to it. "By the way, how are your sister and niece?"

"Perfect. It was a struggle for a few months, but they're back and better than ever. Jackie even decided to play soccer this season, and is loving it." Such pride filled his voice as he spoke of his niece. One day Eden would be a fantastic dad to a lucky kid.

"I'm happy to hear it. Maybe we could catch a game of hers sometime. Or you could bring them both for dinner and she could play with my kids." While they shared a bit more small talk, I snuck back upstairs to finish getting ready.

CHAPTER 13
EDEN

All of my moments with Adam felt like firsts. Nothing we had done was out of the ordinary for me, yet somehow his smile made the sky brighter, his kisses made my toes tingle for hours later, and his cologne got my blood pumping. The scent lingered in this room, and on Maggie too because I noticed it when she gave me a hug.

Sitting downstairs on the couch, I waited while Maggie went upstairs to "hurry him up," in her words. Out of the corner of my eye, I spotted an admirer peeking through the stair posts. It was Amber, the shrieking wonder, and I only hoped she wouldn't be frightened of my spotting her. Already sporting a twinge of a headache brought on by nerves, I couldn't handle her high-pitched sound.

"Hi," she whispered softly from across the room.

Her tiny hand raised in a wave, so I waved back and invited her over. Drowning in an oversized T-shirt, she stumbled forward and I caught her in time to lift her onto the couch.

"My Uncle Adam says I can talk to you. He says you're not a stranger, you're his friend. I like your hair. Can I touch it?"

Most people weren't allowed to come near my hair without proper certification, but I made an exception. Bowing my head, I waited as she patted the top where I had spiked it up into a fauxhawk for the date. Giggles filled the room as she continued to pat it. My anal-retentive side was worried I'd have a flat hairdo by the time Adam came downstairs.

"Little stink, what are you doing to my friend's hair?" Coming down the stairs, Adam was dressed in khakis and a navy blue fitted shirt. With his arms crossed, the shirt sleeves were straining against the bulge of his biceps.

"He said I could touch it, Uncle Adam. I asked nicely."

"As long as you said please." Amber turned toward me wearing a sheepish look, ready to confess, but I covered for her.

"She was very polite when she asked me." Not going to lie for the kid, but she had been polite, even without the please added.

Sweeping Amber up in his arms, he held her over his head and upside down. "You better run upstairs to get your bath before your momma comes down to find you." More giggles were followed by tiny footsteps running up the stairs. My attention was now focused on Adam's face. He had shaved the scruff, and I reached up to feel the soft skin. Closing his eyes, he grinned as I molested his face. "I was afraid you'd miss the scruff. Seems like I was mistaken."

"You look good either way in my opinion." Pulling my hand away, I had to take a deep breath to keep from jerking him forward for a kiss. Every nerve in my body tingled as I stood so close to him.

Bending his elbow, he asked, "Are you ready for our date?" I linked my arm with his and eagerly nodded. "Where would you like to go?"

"You asked me out. It's only fair for you to decide where to." Decision-making had never been my forte anyway. Offering to drive, Adam promised I wouldn't be disappointed in his choice but refused to tell me our destination.

"At least I know you're not a vegan or vegetarian. I've seen you eat meat," I said. Adam snorted with laughter and wiggled his eyebrows for a moment before I caught on. "I mean because you fixed chicken that time. I need to be careful what I say around you, ya big perv."

"The biggest. And proud of it." A flick of his shirt gave a faux show of ego.

An hour later, we were sitting down to dinner at a steakhouse Adam said was one of his favorites. Ordering an appetizer to share, we decided on the bison meatballs and both snickered when we ordered them as bison balls and had a lot of inappropriate conversation with the waitress containing as much innuendo as possible.

"How are Eve and Jackie?" Popping a ball in his mouth, Adam opened his lips in an O as he breathed out the heat radiating from the fresh meat.

"Back to their old selves. It was a long road. I only moved back to my own place a month ago. Having my own space again has been great. Don't you miss yours?" Living with a woman who wasn't your wife and three kids who weren't yours would have to take a toll eventually. It would have for me; I liked my personal space too much.

Adam shrugged. "Not really. I enjoy having Mags and the kids around, and I still get a lot of free time. Even more so when Amber starts school. It's nice to have a family to come home to. When I had my own place, it got very lonely." His eyes dipped down to the plate, and his lips turned down into a frown.

"So if you do meet someone you want a long-term relationship with, you'll move out, right?" His attachment to Maggie and the children made me hesitant to hope for a future. If we fell in love—I was halfway there already—I'd want to live together, but not in the house with a woman and three children. I wanted a family of my own one day. Sensing my concern, Adam reached across the table to hold my hand.

"What are you looking for out of this?"

Since I wasn't expecting that to be the question he asked, I wasn't sure what my answer would be. The truth seemed best. Beating around the bush, waiting to see what he wanted or the move he'd make, hadn't worked for us before. New start, new process. "One day I want a family. Whether it be with you or someone else, I'd like to be married, maybe have kids."

"Same here. By the time I'm ready for a step so big, I think Maggie will be able to live on her own. For now, I can't see moving out until there's someone to come home to."

"I can live with that answer. As much as I love my sister and niece, my life can't revolve around them to the point I sacrifice my happiness. I want to make sure you feel the same about Maggie." Even if he didn't direct it toward a future with me, I caught the under-lying implication that he wanted much more than a one-night stand. Adam was who I wanted, now and possibly forever. I knew because no one else had ever captivated my attention the way he did.

Apparently he not only captured my attention, but he also put me in a trance. He waved his hand in front of my face, and I heard a faraway voice say, "Eden?"

Shaking my thoughts away, I noted the worry on Adam's face and I smiled reassuringly. "Sorry, low blood sugar I think. I haven't eaten all day."

"Put some balls in your mouth," Adam teased.

"Out in the middle of the restaurant? You have no shame, Mr. Simmons." Grinning at him, I shook my head.

"Ooh, I like it when you call me mister." A seductive growl rolled from his mouth. Even on an empty stomach, I wanted to forgo food, take him back to my place, and ravish him for the next few hours. But then again, it was good to fuel up before doing strenuous activity. That idea was shot down by his next words. "I'd love to do unmentionable things to you tonight, but I still think slow is the way to go. Are you going to be satisfied with dinner and the possibility of a goodnight kiss?"

"Satisfied is probably not the best word, but I think you're worth the wait." Reaching across the table, I placed my hand over his. "I mean, I've waited six months to see your handsome face again. It should be a breeze to wait a little longer for more."

Adam squeezed my hand, his cheeks filled with a

blush. He'd never come off as the blushing type to me; it was cute to see a moment of vulnerability.

For the rest of dinner, we laughed and tried our best to avoid too much flirting, but at times it was inevitable. Adam picked up the check and took my hand to lead me out the door. We got a few odd looks, which was normal considering our hometown, but I ignored them. "If you're not tired, I thought we could hang out a little longer?" he said.

"I'm not tired in the least. What do you have in mind?"

"Come back to my place? Curl up on the couch and watch movies?" The idea of lying in Adam's arms all night was definitely appealing, but....

"With Maggie and the kids? Why not come to my place? You could sleep over."

"At my house, we'd have supervision so we can stick to taking things slow." Although he had a valid point, I wanted time alone with him.

"We're adults, we can control ourselves." Tugging on his arm, I grinned. "Come back to my place. Please?" Batting my eyes at him, I watched while he fought against his better judgment before finally agreeing to my suggestion.

CHAPTER 14
ADAM

Cozy but small, Eden's apartment had a certain charm. Most of his furniture appeared handmade, due to the intricate detail and subtle flaws in the wood, which meant it was probably made by him. It had a unique, artistic quality about it I'd never seen before. While Eden excused himself to the restroom, I stepped closer to examine his work.

Tracing my fingers across the sculpted wood, I admired the elaborate carvings in the back of the chair. His talents in the garden were superb, but I'd never imagined he'd have even more talent. When he'd mentioned carpentry, I pictured simple wood construction, straight lines, a country feel. There was nothing simple about his work.

"You look a little too comfortable with my chair

there." I had been admiring the piece so closely I'd missed him coming back in the room.

"Is this some of your work?" Eden nodded. "It's gorgeous."

"Thanks. If it's made of wood in this apartment, it's mine." An odd crinkle around his eye formed as he seemed to notice the opening he'd left for a sex-related comment and awaited my joke.

With a wink, I responded, "I'm going to let that one slide." Now that I knew he'd made most of the furniture, I walked around the room to admire other pieces. "Where do you do your woodworking?"

"My work machinery stays at Eve's house. I rented her garage to store it. Mostly I did it to help her with the bills. Being a single mom hasn't been easy for her. Her pride won't let her take money from me without giving me something in return."

The coffee table was made of oak with Celtic carvings outlining the edge of the table and trees carved into either side. "This looks like it was inspired by *Lord of the Rings*. Is that too much of my nerd side showing?"

"Not for me. It was inspired by it in a way. Besides the woodwork in the movies, the scenery is enough to...." His eyes had grown cloudy as he stared off dreamily, and when his words trailed off, he blushed. "Sorry, I think my nerd was showing there. What movie do you want to watch? I've got a small selection in the back or we can scroll through Netflix."

"I know we're supposed to avoid this, but—" Leaning forward, I brushed my lips against Eden's. "I missed the taste of these lips," I whispered against his mouth. He parted them, allowing my tongue to slip past. His hands grazed my sides as he grasped my shirt, pulling me closer. Moving my head to his shoulder, I wrapped my arms around his waist, clasping my hands behind his back. "It feels good to be here with you."

CHAPTER 15
EDEN

"So, tell me all about it!" Eve pulled a chair out next to me at the table, scooted close, and placed her chin on her hands, eagerly awaiting details of my date with Adam.

"It was nice."

Her mouth fell open, eyes rolled back in her head, and she mocked a loud snore. "Nice is boring. I want the dirt. So spill."

"We had dinner. Then he came back to the house, and he kissed me. After the kiss, we spent the evening curled up on the couch watching movies. Adam fell asleep during the third movie and started snoring lightly. It sounded like a purring kitten. It was adorable." He had been lying against me at the time. My legs fell asleep before I did, which made things a bit uncomfortable, but having his body against mine felt so good, the pain of not being able to move became barely noticeable in comparison. "I snapped a picture." Opening my phone, I showed her a photo of Adam asleep with his head against my chest. "I know it's a little stalker-ish, but I couldn't help it."

"Sneaky, but I would have done the same thing. Nothing else happened after the kiss?

"Nope. We're taking it slow for now. This morning we made plans for a second date." Adam had woken up in my arms, glanced up at me through hooded eyes, and grinned. He said he slept better than he had in years. After a good-morning kiss, he said he couldn't wait to see me again. Since he had to work the next few nights, I would have to wait almost a week for our date. Six days might as well have been a year, with how anxious I was to see him again.

Sniffing the air, Eve's forehead creased. "Are you wearing a new cologne?"

"It's Adam's cologne. From where he slept on me. I didn't stop to grab a shower this morning because I would have been late meeting you. I like the scent though." Pulling my shirt up to my nose, I took a whiff, closed my eyes, and smiled as Adam's face appeared in my mind.

"You've got it bad. I haven't seen you this in love since…." I could tell she wanted to say Earl, but neither of us had mentioned his name in years. "I like seeing you happy. It warms my heart, little brother. You've been the best stand-in dad for Jackie. With everything you've done to make sure I'm taken care of, I've been hoping you'd meet someone to put a smile on your face like the one you have today.

After spending the day with Eve, I went back home to my apartment. Lying on the couch, I flipped on the television to find one of the movies we'd watched the night before. It was called *Mystic Pizza*, one of Julia Roberts's first movies. I could recite this one by heart, I'd seen it so many times. Now it had new memories for me as I closed my eyes and imagined Adam being there with me. It was going to be a long six days.

Six days later, I stood in front of Adam once more at his house. Tonight it was my turn to pick the plans, and I chose a restaurant close to my house. Dinner went smoothly, never a moment of awkwardness between us. It was as if we'd known each other for years. Throughout the meal, Adam had played footsie with me underneath the table. After the appetizer, before we ordered our meal, his foot glided up the inside of my leg, grazing my thigh before rubbing against my cock. A mischievous grin appeared on his face as I bit my lip to hold back the moan I desperately wanted to release.

"We have to stop flirting, because I could eat my arm right now I'm so hungry, but my dick is trying to convince me to get out of here with you," he declared. It was good to know Adam and I were on the same page. Tonight would be a night for the record books if the passion was anything like our last two encounters.

"Let's compromise. We can share a meal now, go back to my place and work up more of an appetite, and order pizza after?" Appearing to like the idea, Adam waved the waitress down and ordered the club sandwich and asked for two side salads. I burst into laughter, scaring the waitress, who started to turn away quickly. At the same time, we called out, "No onions on the salads."

"You ordered the quickest meal on the menu. Nice move." Our food arrived in less than ten minutes. Splitting the sandwich in half, we each scarfed down our portions as well as the salads. Adam felt an explanation was needed when we flagged the waitress down once more for the check. "Sorry, we're late for a movie." It seemed a valid enough excuse to use, but I was pretty positive she saw right through us, what with the wink and fist bump she gave Adam. My cheeks reddened with embarrassment.

"Damn, you're hot when you blush." Cocking an eyebrow, his ran his tongue across his lips.

Lowering my voice to a whisper, I trailed my fingers along his arm. "If you don't quit giving me compliments or doing that growl thing, I'm going to come right here."

"Challenge accepted." Another growl followed his words.

Adam paid the check after agreeing to let me pick it up next time. Hearing him mention a next time sent the butterflies fluttering in my stomach. When we reached the car, Adam grabbed my arm and spun me around, pressing me against the door. Warm, wet lips brushed against mine as a hand moved to my hip. He tugged at my belt, pulling me closer, and his hips bucked against me.

Tongues dancing in a hot, passionate, demanding kiss, it was as though I couldn't bring him close enough to satisfy me. Opening the back door, he motioned me inside, then climbed in and lay above me. We ground our erections together, the friction driving me wild with passion. "I want to fuck you," Adam growled against my throat as his tongue trailed across my collarbone. I gasped at a sudden sharp pain, and knew he'd left a hickey on me. Marking his territory. It drove me wild to have him claim me.

"My place, not here." Our first time couldn't be in

public. Plus, I wanted to have plenty of time and space to have my way with him. There wasn't enough room to fuck him half the ways I wanted to.

"I almost took you over the table in that fucking restaurant. It'll take too long to drive there." Adam's impatience had my cock eagerly twitching.

"It's only twenty minutes."

"My dick will fall off by then." Frantically fidgeting with my zipper, he pulled my dick free and wrapped his mouth around it. *Fuck.* The sheer power of his lips had me ready to shoot my load, but I desperately held back. I wanted to enjoy this pleasure, to freeze this moment in time for as long as possible. His mouth gripped tighter, pulling in longer strokes, weakening my resistance. Wrapping my fingers in his hair, I held on to his head as I thrust forward into his mouth, releasing my seed with a gasp and a shudder. He licked his lips as he sat up, and I pulled Adam back down on top of me, our tongues once more in an erotic dance. Tasting myself on his lips made me want him even more. "To my house, now. It's my turn to show you my skills."

Growling with lusty approval, Adam moved to the front passenger seat. The next twenty minutes felt like hours. During the drive, Adam placed his hand on my thigh, gently massaging it, slowly making me hard no matter how I tried to fight it. At one point, he leaned over to trail his tongue along my neck. Grabbing my earlobe between his teeth, he tugged gently. Pressing his lips to my ear, he whispered, "I want you, Eden."

"Just a few more minutes," I said, mostly reminding myself.

The parking lot to the condos was about fifty feet from my front door; today it might as well have been a mile for how long it seemed to take for us to get inside. Before I could get out of the car, Adam had tugged me over to him for a kiss. Not a simple peck on the lips, either. It started with his tongue gliding across my bottom lip just before he sucked on it, then covered my mouth with his. Our tongues mingled. Palms pressed against his cheeks, I held him in place, not ready to let him go.

Finally breaking apart, we spilled out of the car and rushed up toward my condo. Adam pressed against my back, his mouth working its way across my neck, causing me great difficulty when trying to concentrate. Fumbling with the key, I felt like a boy on prom night trying to find the correct hole to put it in. A slew of curse words, followed by a shove of my shoulder, and the door flew open. I kicked the door closed behind us, not bothering to lock it. Adam's cock was rubbing against my back. I'd showed him mine; it was time for him to show me his.

Shirts flew off, cascading to the floor. His hand

cupped the back of my neck, jerking me forward into a kiss. Tugging at his belt loop, I led him to the bedroom. It was my turn to take charge. I playfully shoved Adam onto the bed, and he bounced up a little as he hit the mattress. Desire filled his eyes and colored his cheeks. Straddling him, I reached to undo his belt. His dick begged to be let free, and I was granting its wish. Soon I would show little Adam who was boss.

The monstrous beast sprang free as I unzipped his pants. Part of me wanted to scream, "Release the Kracken!" at the sight of the animal; there was nothing *little* about him. Switching between pitcher and catcher has always been my thing. It's never been my style to stick with one position. I enjoy changing things up. At the moment, the thought of being catcher made me a little fearful. I'd never been with someone as large as Adam.

"You're staring at my dick like it's Jaws coming for revenge. It won't bite." With fuck-me eyes staring me down, I licked my lips in anticipation.

"I'm not so sure about that. Have you seen this thing?" Placing my hand at my mouth, I wondered if I could stretch it enough to please him fully. Even if I couldn't take it all in, I'd give it the best possible effort.

"Thank you," Adam said, winking. "Don't you want a taste?" To entice me, he wrapped his hand around his dick, fingers close to touching, and began to stroke himself.

Goddamn, he's hot.

It was so sexy watching him touch himself in front of me. Part of me wanted to watch him, while the other part was anxious for a taste. "Fuck yeah." And I dove down, thinking "Towanda!" the entire way. It was a word from one of my favorite movies, used when doing something wild and crazy, and it seemed incredibly appropriate for this moment. It was a long stretch of a journey, wrapping my mouth around the girth and then taking the length as far into my throat as I could without gagging.

"Faster, Eden." Adam growled, pushing upward with his lower half.

"Mall be BJ." Mumbling around his size was like trying to talk with a mouth full of water. Going faster would be like trying to swallow a banana without chewing.

Adam sat up on his elbows. "What?"

Moving my mouth, I said, "Call me Eden." In the moment, it seemed stupid to correct him. I'd let him get away with calling me Eden many times since we met. Mostly it was an excuse to give my mouth a break.

I ran my tongue along the tip and licked the taste of precum off my lips. He wanted it fast, I'd give it to him. Using my hand to make up for the depth, I stroked him from the bottom, my mouth meeting my hand with each stroke. With my free hand, I cupped his balls, stroking them back and forth, occasionally stopping to suck and lick them.

Soft moans of ecstasy were all I could hear from Adam. Pulling out my secret weapon, I swirled my tongue around the tip, continuing down, taking him into the back of my throat, humming a tune as I backed away and gave his balls a squeeze. A low, guttural moan turned into a scream of pleasure. Spilling his sweet seed down my throat, Adam tensed and his face contorted, eyes closed with his mouth making a perfect O.

Rolling over onto his stomach, Adam got on his knees with his ass in the air. Spreading his cheeks with his hands, he glanced back at me and begged, "Fuck me, Eden." He didn't have to ask twice.

I squirted lube onto my index and middle fingers then slid them into his ass, readying him for my cock. Tightness squeezing my fingers as I slid them inside made my dick rise to the occasion, ready for more thrill.

Lubing up my cock, I gave his ass cheek a smack, to which Adam cried out, "Do it again, baby." It was impossible to tell this man no. Another smack to his cheek in the same spot left a pale pink mark. "More," he begged with a moan. Smacking the spot, I watched the ripple of skin redden more as Adam growled with desire. Firmly grasping his ass with both hands, I slipped my lubed, condom-covered cock inside his warm, tight ass. Once I was inside, I gave him another smack before I slowly moved in and out. "Fuck me harder," Adam cried out. Damn, he was bossy in bed, but his wish was my command. Fisting the sheets, he rocked back and forth as I slammed into him repeatedly.

Between the fast pace and Adam's screams of pleasure, I couldn't hold back my orgasm. My balls tightened, and with one last thrust, waves of pleasure rippled over my body as I slowly pulled out.

I collapsed beside Adam on the bed, and he rolled over, wrapping his arm across my chest. "Without a doubt, best sex of my life." Soft fingers danced across my skin, running through the light smattering of hair on my chest. "I could fall in love with you so easily, Eden James." That small sentence was the sweetest and scariest thing anyone had ever said to me.

CHAPTER 16
ADAM

Fuck me twice and leave me smiling. I'd used the phrase before to display shock about happy news, but today the sentence had a different meaning. After cuddling for a few hours, we woke up starved for one another and went another round.

I'd told Eden an untruth when I said I could fall in love with him. The truth was, I was already there. Eden was the epitome of my ideal soul mate. It was something I'd thought a lot about, especially after watching Maggie and Donovan's love story unfold.

Nothing ever fazed those two. From the moment they came together, love was all they had and all they wanted. Donovan's diagnosis made them stronger instead of tearing them down. Once, they'd shared their secret with me: Pick your battles. They lived by the motto. If it's not worth fighting about, don't.

Maggie said she'd get annoyed with Donovan, but she'd count to twenty in her mind while ticking off the reasons she loved him against the reason she was mad. Every time, the love won out. Neither of them knew how much they inspired me.

Lying beside me, Eden slept peacefully. Gazing at him, I memorized the slope of his nose, the shape of his eyes, the curve of his jaw, the swell of his plump pink lips—lips that tasted better than any chocolate or dessert I'd ever had.

Brushing his hair away from his face, I bent down to breathe him in. His hair smelled like apples from the shampoo I spotted in his shower earlier this evening. Pressing my nose against his neck, I appreciated the musky scent of cologne mixed with sweat that was purely Eden. Lips brushing his earlobe, I whispered, "Are you awake?" No answer, no movement or smile. I tried one more time. "Eden?" Nothing. "I love you," came out in an almost inaudible whisper compared to the other two tries. Fear gripped me as he stirred in his sleep. He rolled over, his hand flopping across my shoulder as he released a long, hot, stale breath in my face. I coughed to catch my own breath. Morning breath wasn't attractive on anyone. Still, I lay facing him so I wouldn't miss a moment.

"Are you staring at me?" Eden mumbled without opening his eyes. "I feel creeper stares." The sleepy growl of his voice was getting me ready for round, well, I'd lost count.

Answering with laughter, I leaned closer and whispered in my best creepy voice, "I'm watching you."

"Freak." Eyes still closed, he tried to hold back a grin without success. "You wore me out last night. I need sleep."

"Me? You were the one smacking my ass so much I can barely sit." Not that I was complaining. I'd walk around with his handprint permanently attached to my ass if it meant more dates ending the same way.

"Good thing we're in bed then. And I remember you asking for it, often." Eden's eyes popped open and he drank me in. The desire in his gaze made my cock take notice and rise to the occasion.

Last night I'd let him dominate me; tonight, or today, would be my turn. "Tonight, I want to give you a spanking you'll never forget."

"What makes you think I don't have plans tonight? It's possible I have a date." Even knowing he was teasing, it hurt my heart to think of him with another man.

"Really? Another date? I don't think so." My voice was full of confidence. I wanted him to know how much I wanted from this date. He should know I was all his and I wanted him to be mine. After last night, he was mine as far as I was concerned.

"What does that mean?" His eyebrow rose in curiosity, mouth widening in a grin.

"It means—" I sat up and moved above him, propping myself above his body, leaning close to his face. "—you're mine." Our lips crashed together, and I felt his approval of my claim against my leg.

Pulling away from the kiss, Eden smiled up at me and replied, "I am." There was no question in his tone, only agreement. Hot, submissive, fucking agreement. He was mine.

For the rest of the day, I showed him my dominant side.

CHAPTER 17
EDEN

Worn out was putting it mildly. Adam stayed at my house for three days, since he had no shifts scheduled. During the day, he went home to care for the kids, but was back at my house each night when I came home.

Each night was a different welcome-home surprise. Night one, a romantic dinner was on the table when I came home. Lights off, nothing but a soft glow of candlelight coming from the kitchen. The table was set with candles, a vase of roses, and plates full of finger foods. Chicken nuggets, cheese sticks, strawberries, grapes; it was a strange combination of foods. "What is this?"

"It's sadly what you had in your refrigerator. I would've gone to the store, but I knew you'd be home before I made it back and I wanted to surprise you. Even if it's a dish of appetizers, I thought if anyone can make this sexy and romantic it's us. Right?" At first I didn't answer him because the gesture was so sweet I had no words. "Wait, maybe one more thing to add to the sexy." Pulling his shirt over his head, he threw it across the room to the couch. Hand on the chair, he raised his other arm and flexed his muscle. "Now is it full-on sexy?"

"Oh yeah," I breathed, taking in his beautiful form I'd never grow tired of gazing upon. "I'm overdressed, it seems." And filthy, as I'd worked three yards that day and brought home the evidence to prove it all over my clothes and skin. "And I'm in desperate need of a shower."

Blowing out the candles and covering the plates with napkins, Adam held out his hand. "I'm no longer hungry for food. Let's do the shower thing instead."

Night number two, I found Adam sitting naked on the couch with a red bow on his cock. "No dinner tonight?" I asked as I walked in the door. No complaints from me. It was just a way to start the conversation.

Without moving, he patted the seat next to him. "I liked our spontaneity last night and thought we could repeat that dinner instead." Eyes dropping to the bow, I watched intently as his hand stroked his cock.

"Why don't I watch you first, and then we'll clean up." Biting his lip, Adam continued stroking. I reached forward enough to untie the bow, sliding it slowly across his skin. Laying his head back, he sucked air through his teeth as the soft ribbon caressed his skin and his hand moved faster. I licked my lips, wanting to taste him, the sweet, salty flavor of Adam, but watching him pleasure himself was so hot.

As I watched him, I'd begun removing my clothes. When he came, he spilled his load all over his chest. Leaning forward, I tasted his lips before taking his hand and guiding him to the bedroom. I tied the ribbon from earlier around his eyes. The pleasure I got from watching, he'd experience through a different sense.

And night three was my favorite. It had been a stressful day workwise when an entire batch of wood came in knotted to the point of being unusable. Sending it back would cost me a week's worth of time, making it impossible to reach my deadline.

Due to the delay, I had to discount the furniture by 30 percent so I didn't lose the customer. On the way home to see Adam, I'd gotten a speeding ticket for going five over in an obvious speed trap in town. It didn't seem like saying, "I'm trying to get home to see my hot-ass boyfriend" would get me out of the ticket.

For the first time in three days, I reached the house and wished Adam wasn't there, because I knew I wouldn't be great company. Walking in the door, head hung low, I heard music coming from the bedroom. Rolling my eyes up toward the ceiling, I took a deep breath and hoped my mood would improve when I laid eyes on him.

Dropping my keys in a blue shiny bowl next to the door, I kicked my shoes off and pushed them to the side. Strolling down to the bedroom, I took another deep breath and stepped inside. The image in front of me heightened my mood almost instantly.

Adam stood wearing a pair of black boxer briefs with a bow tie around his neck. Carrying a towel on his arm, he motioned to the bed. "Tonight I am at your beck and call. Get comfortable in bed. I'll bring your dinner to you, and afterward you'll enjoy a massage. Sensual or relaxing—your choice."

"What's this all about?" Not a criticism, but I was curious how he knew I would need pampering.

"Eve called and said you'd had a bad day. She knew you wouldn't want to tell me and thought you might push me away instead of confiding in me. I want to make sure it doesn't happen. So tonight, it's all about you, baby."

"I love you, Adam." I waited anxiously to see what his response would be as his eyes widened at my confession. Either we'd end this night with amazing sex or I would scare him away and it would simply end.

Any anxiety I had was put to ease the moment he grabbed my face and pulled me in for a kiss. "I love you too," he whispered against my lips. For years I was sure I'd never find a man who could give me everything I wanted and satisfy my needs without trying to control me. Adam and I were on equal footing.

For the rest of the evening, he did exactly as he'd promised and made it all about me. Everything bad about the day washed away as he pampered me and in turn let me pamper him a bit, per my request.

"I've told you about my past. Tell me a little about yours. How did you tell your parents you're gay? With them being so religious, I can't imagine it was easy." Adam's question surprised me, though it really shouldn't have.

"My coming out moment came after a lot of soul searching. I could stand in the middle of a crowded room and shout it out to a group of strangers, but the thought of telling my own parents terrified me. Something, no, it was someone, convinced me it was time to tell them." Glancing away from Adam, I wondered if it was the right moment to talk about another man I'd loved. He had confided in me about his history with Donovan.

"Was it Eve who convinced you?" He ran his thumb across my palm. Looking in his eyes, I found comfort in talking about the past.

"No. Eve wanted me to, but there was someone else who pushed me. Earl was my lab partner in chemistry. We bonded over homework assignments and cursing our parents for not thinking before strapping us with these awful names. One night, after school in the library, we both bent down to pick up a pencil that rolled off the table. When we both reached for it, I started to laugh it off, but Earl surprised me with a kiss. It was my first male kiss. I was in sheer panic, looking to be sure no one had spotted us." Adam brought my hand up to his mouth and kissed it.

"For days after, I steered clear of Earl, but one day we were alone again. He brought up the kiss. What began as a slightly awkward conversation ended with a passionate second lip-lock. Suddenly I understood the passion I'd read about and seen in film. With girls, I'd always thought sex must be overrated, because I barely enjoyed a kiss, but with Earl it was intense, unforgettable pleasure. When I came, I saw fireworks and heard violins in the background. Earl was my first everything as a gay man. He told me he loved me just before graduation, giving me the courage to come out to my parents."

"Though I don't like thinking about you with other guys, I'm glad Earl was able to give you the courage. And damn, I can't blame him for hating that name."

Positioning himself above me, Adam leaned down to capture my lips. "I want to make you see fireworks."

"With you, it's much bigger explosions." Slipping my tongue through his lips, I reveled in the flavor of Adam, my favorite taste of late.

When he rested beside me again, he said, "So tell me more about how it went with your parents."

"I waited a few days after graduation to allow the high to wear off and for Eve to return home for the summer. We fixed my parents supper, sat down at the table, and Eve said, 'Eden has something to share with you.'"

"Nice of her to give you the opening." If Eve hadn't brought it up, I might have chickened out.

"Without pause, or time to freak out, I said, 'I'm gay.' It was followed by gazes of judgment and criticism, or at least I interpreted them as such. Neither of them said anything. I was greeted with blank stares. To get a reaction I said, 'Just kidding. I contracted a rare disease and I have eight months to live.' To this my father started to tear up, so I said, 'Dad, I'm not dying. I'm just gay. Is that better?'"

"You thought telling him you were dying was a better idea? That's harsh, but I suppose I can understand that to a point." Still eagerly listening, Adam ran his fingers through my hair as I continued my story.

"My father stood up and walked over to my chair.

He'd never raised a hand to me in his life, but I braced myself for a slap as if it were a common response. Instead, he leaned forward, wrapped his arms around my shoulders, and hugged me tight. 'I'm definitely glad you're not dying. And I'm so proud you finally felt comfortable enough to share this news with us.' I expected the news to make my dad different around me, but his hug was the same strength as always. His words, his lack of surprise, were genuine. Dreaming up a better reaction would be utterly impossible."

"Wow, not what I would have expected either."

"For so long, I hid who I was from everyone, including myself, but then it was like I announced to my parents I'd gotten into college. They were proud, relieved even. My mother said they'd suspected it for quite some time. And then they asked me what made me admit it. So I told them about Earl. Don't get me wrong, my parents didn't jump up and start wearing big signs that said, 'My son likes boys!' or decorating everything in rainbow colors. They were there in the best ways that counted. Never once did they attempt to 'fix' me or insinuate I was anything different than the man they raised."

"It's a better story than some end up with, especially when coming from religious families." Adam looked away for a moment in thought before asking, "What happened with Earl?"

"Earl and I stayed together for a few years after high school. Our third year of college, we went our separate ways. Our breakup was a mutual decision and we agreed to remain friends. For a while we stuck to it, and then life got in the way." Earl's mother had come between us, but in truth, there was no hope for a future there. We'd grown apart even before she'd convinced him I wasn't good enough.

As we lay in bed together, limbs intertwined, I needed to know how long this would last. And I wanted to veer the subject away from Earl. "It's been three days since you've been home with Maggie. Don't you miss spending time with her?" The last thing I wanted was to make him resent me for coming between him and his best friend.

"I do miss her. Since I'm on the night shift tomorrow, I was going to spend some time with her during the day. Give you a break from me for a day or two." In past relationships, personal space had been an issue for me. Earl, even with his mother's interference, had been clingy almost to the point of smothering. We'd had to make rules about taking time apart to keep us from getting annoyed with the other. With Adam, the thought of being apart filled me with loneliness.

"I'm not sure I ever need a break from you, but I understand you want to spend time with her. I want you to keep your life how it was and not let me interfere." Not the most honest answer, since he could move in with me and I wouldn't complain.

"That's almost impossible to do. You weren't in my life before. Now that you are, I want to devote time to getting to know you even better." Adam stroked his finger across my cheek as he spoke. "I need to know everything about you, Eden James."

"You've seen parts of me no one else ever has."

"Or ever will again if I have anything to say about it." His possessive words caused me to bite my lip, holding back the grin of pleasure. No one else could possess me the way he did.

"Once you and Maggie have some time together, I'd like to schedule a dinner where you can meet Eve and Jackie officially." Eve had been begging me to bring Adam over. She was appalled knowing he'd only ever seen her in a hospital bed with a swollen face, looking the worst she'd ever looked. No matter how many times I'd told her she was still beautiful, she wouldn't believe her little brother.

A wide, gleaming grin meeting sparkling, joyful eyes let me know he approved of the idea. "Maybe we could have a dinner with Maggie and all the kids too?"

"I'd love it," I replied genuinely. Since I always seemed to miss the two oldest kids, it would be interesting to see the rest of the family. My only hope was they didn't all scream as loudly as Amber.

COMING HOME TO AN EMPTY HOUSE HAD BEEN MUCH lonelier after getting used to Adam staying with me the last few days. I had grown accustomed to his smile greeting me at the door. After he spent the day with Maggie, he planned to come to my house on his way to work for a few minutes. I'd take every minute he'd give me. Unfortunately, when he stopped by, it didn't go the way I hoped.

With only a half hour to spare, Adam came through the door and wrapped his arms around me, giving me a quick kiss before telling me about his day. During their day together, Maggie had admitted to him she'd barely slept due to Amber having nightmares. She asked if he could come home for a bit to help her get some sleep. Apologizing profusely and begging me not to hate her, she was more worried about our love life than her own sanity, according to Adam.

It must have run in the household, because Adam began his apologies from the minute he packed his stuff. Assuring him I was fine and we'd be back together soon, I sent him on his way and promised I'd see him on Thursday to work on their yard. Sharing a man with anyone wasn't my strong suit; in fact, it was one of the things that led to my breakup with Earl. He was a bit too much of a mama's boy. It was nice when a man wanted to take care of his mother and even put her first in his life, but there was a line, which would be when your mother started dictating how fast you moved in a relationship.

Every move forward we made, he practically had to get permission from his mother before asking. Our breakup was mutual and I didn't hate him at all, but it still set a precedent for future relationships. At times I even missed him in my life; he was a good friend before things turned romantic.

Ex-boyfriends and lovers hadn't been much of a conversation between Adam and me except to let the other know we'd always practiced safe sex. Talking about my relationship with Earl in detail wasn't something I was ready to do.

Life had other plans, though.

Waking up bright and early the next morning, I had a message on my phone from an unknown number. When I pressed the voice mail playback button, I fell back into a chair in shock. Earl's voice rang out through my phone, sounding devastated. "Can you call me? I need a friend" was all the message said.

Four years since we'd spoken, and he called me? Knowing what desperation sounded like in his voice, I called him back immediately. "Eden?" he answered, voice gravelly and low.

"What's wrong?" Dread dropped into my stomach

like I'd swallowed a ten-pound weight. Drama was something I avoided as much as possible. And a call from an ex-boyfriend seemed like an open invitation for drama.

"Mom died last week, and I'm having a hard time getting out of bed. It was a heart attack in the middle of the night. Nothing I could have done to save her." Halfway through the words, he began to sob.

"Earl, I'm so sorry. What can I do?" After a week, I knew she'd already been buried and offering to help with that was futile.

"I know it's asking a lot, but I need a friend. Is it possible for me to come visit you for a few days? I'd invite you here, but I need to get away." My head screamed no, but my heart remembered how much I'd loved this man once, and I couldn't deny such a simple request. His next words made the guilt even worse. "I don't have anyone else, Eden. Please?"

"Absolutely. Just tell me when you want to come, and I'll be ready."

He grew quiet for a moment, so I knew he'd left something out. I waited patiently, and he finally said, "I'm already in town. If you give me your address, I can let you know how far away."

Rattling off my address, I waited for him to enter it into his GPS so he could give me an estimated time of arrival.

"I'll see you in thirty minutes. Thanks, Eden, I can't wait to see you."

That makes one of us at least. The lead weight filling my stomach hadn't subsided. To be honest, I wanted to see Earl to know how his life was going. Then again, when he'd said there was no one else he could turn to, it didn't give me much hope he'd been living happily.

I tried to call Adam, but Maggie said he was still at work. What I needed to tell him could wait until he clocked out. Only twenty-five minutes to go, and I had to grab a shower and get dressed. Hair still soaking wet, I had just thrown on a pair of shorts and a T-shirt when the doorbell rang.

In high school and most of college, Earl had a body that made Sheldon Cooper from *The Big Bang Theory* look pudgy. The typical nerd with large, thick-framed glasses who wore superhero shirts and never cared if he wore socks with sandals was standing at my door looking like he'd hulked out. Biceps strained against a tight V-neck T-shirt tucked into a pair of dark blue skinny jeans tucked into a pair of black cowboy boots.

"Earl?" I choked out, sure this had to be a mistake. But even before I heard his voice, I knew it was him behind those giant brown eyes. Wrapping his arms around me, Earl began to sob against my neck.

Staring at a pile of luggage sitting on the porch next to him, I wondered how long he planned to stay.

"I'm sorry to blubber all over you." Earl pulled away, wiping his eyes. "You look good, Eden."

"It's Eden, remember?" Only Adam got away with calling me Eden now. "Have a seat on the couch. Coffee?"

"Alcohol would be best, but I suppose it's too early. For now, I'll take coffee."

"Black no sugar," we said simultaneously. Throwing him a wink, I watched him blush as a smile crept across his face. Suddenly I was taken back to five years ago when our relationship was strong and all I wanted was to spend time with him. Pouring coffee beans into the grinder, I pushed the button, letting my mind wander in the midst of the noise. It couldn't hurt to let him stay one night so we could catch up. But I needed to talk to Adam as soon as possible.

"Need some help?"

"Motherfu—" My life flashed before my eyes as Earl came into the kitchen and snuck up on me. Pointing at the cabinet to the right, I took a deep breath and said without thinking, "Grab two cups while I finish my heart attack." I cringed, hoping I hadn't offended Earl with the heart attack joke.

"I can't believe you still have this." He held up a coffee mug that he must have dug into the back of the cabinet for, and I cringed. It was a plain black mug with a red heart and letters that spelled out I heart NY.

Our first romantic getaway was to New York City, and we'd each bought a coffee mug for the other.

"It's just a cup, no sense throwing it away." It didn't seem to hurt his feelings too much. Nodding in agreement, he placed the mugs next to the pot, and I filled them up.

We sat down at the dining room table. "Tell me what happened with your mom."

He blew softly across the top of his mug, trying to cool the boiling hot liquid. Loud slurps followed, and he gasped at the heat. Chuckling, I said, "Same ole Earl. You never were patient enough to let it cool. I think you burned several layers off your tongue over the years."

"Patience has never been my virtue. You always read me the riot act over it too. You used to tell me you had plans for that tongue and I better not burn it clean off." Awkward glances were exchanged, and he straightened his posture. "Um, yeah, about Mom. It's been tough, man."

"Had she had previous heart attacks?" Back when I knew her, I couldn't remember her being anything but healthy. We'd had dinner at her house a few times, and she always cooked grilled chicken with steamed veggies. It was the only thing she knew how to cook well, according to Earl.

"Nope. You know how healthy she ate, so it makes

no sense. After we broke up, I moved in with her. Did you know?"

"Honestly, we may have been Facebook friends, but I avoided looking at your page. It was too hard." Other than the occasional moments where I missed him and would go to look at his pictures, or comment once or twice on a post to let him know I was there, I avoided his page as much as possible. I never looked for where he was living or working, but for a while I searched for the elusive relationship status.

"I haven't followed yours either. The thought of you dating a new guy shredded me." Peering over his cup of coffee, he cocked his eyebrow. "*Is there a special guy in your life?*"

"Yes. It's new, but he's pretty special. Are you seeing someone?" *If he says yes, this evening will be much easier to get through.*

"Not in a while. I dated one guy for a little bit, but he had some family issues that tore us apart. Go figure." Strange how his only relationship after me ended in the same way but with the opposite family causing issues.

"How did you meet your guy?" Talking about Adam with my ex-boyfriend didn't seem like a smart idea. Our relationship was personal, and I wasn't ready to share it with anyone, especially Earl. Changing the subject seemed a better move.

"You know I only have one bedroom here. Are you sure you don't want to book a hotel room? My couch isn't so comfy." It was the best excuse I'd been able to come up with since he arrived.

"We could share your bed if you want." Earl winked, waited a moment, and laughed as though he were teasing. "Couch is fine. Like I said, I need a friend right now, and you were the first person I thought of. You know my mother was all the family I had left. And, well, I haven't made any real friends in the last few years. Is your boyfriend the jealous type?"

"Like I said, it's new." Perhaps I should've phrased that differently, because now Earl seemed to have all sorts of hope about our future, based on the rise of his eyebrow and sudden gleam in his eyes.

The next words out of his mouth proved me right. "I always hated the way things ended between us." Reaching over to cover my hand with his, thumb stroking across my skin in circles, he leaned closer. "You are the one who got away for me."

Easing my hand out from under his, I took back a little personal space of my own. "I'm flattered, but I'm serious about this guy." I kept my voice as sympathetic but distant as possible, wanting to let Earl know I was his friend and nothing more.

With a shrug, Earl lifted his cup to his mouth once

more. "When, sorry, *if* it doesn't work out, you know you can call me."

"We were a long time ago, Earl. I've changed since then." Maybe not physically the way he had, but I'd matured a lot in the last four years. Enough that I didn't want to slip back into old habits or beds.

"Doesn't seem like you've changed much to me." Eyes raked over my body. "Still my edible Eden."

Edible Eden was the pet name he gave me back in college. The innuendo made it sexy back then; now it sounded gross, like Hannibal Lector creepy. Especially when he added wiggling eyebrows and licked his lips after saying it.

"I go strictly by Eden now. No pet names" One night was all I was giving him. Tomorrow morning, he had to leave, grieving or not. It may have made me a terrible friend, but we hadn't spoken in years, so I was already a terrible one to begin with.

Nothing could ruin what I had with Adam now. I wouldn't let it. We deserved a good, strong chance at happiness. Every decision I made now could affect it. Since our first date, a little more than a week ago, even a trip to the grocery store had me questioning what Adam would want.

"Would you mind if I took a shower? I've been driving a long time, and I need to clean up." Earl grabbed his luggage from next to the door and reached inside to pull out some clothes.

"Sure, it's down the hall, first door on your left. Towels are in the closet." Earl stretched his arms, his shirt rising to show off the cut just above the waistline of his pants. Time certainly had been good to him.

My phone rang and I grinned to see Adam's name pop up, along with a picture of him in nothing but a towel in my bathroom. He must have programmed his own contact photo into my phone. *Damn, I love him.*

"Hello, gorgeous, and in case you're wondering, I'm talking to the photo on my phone." If he could have seen the goofy grin on my face right then, he'd never doubt my feelings for him.

Chuckling softly, Adam gave a low growl. "I was going to make it a straight dick pic, but I didn't want anyone getting jealous of what you have."

"And what exactly do I have?"

"The hottest doctor boyfriend ever?" Ding! The magic word was used, so we had now made it official. Just the thought made me feel like a teenager again. Grinning widely, I wanted to kick my heels up and do a little happy dance.

"Without a doubt. So, we're exclusive, right?" I needed full disclosure.

Adam grew quiet all of a sudden, worrying me. "I

love you, Eden. I don't say those words to just anyone."

"I love you too."

"Look, I called because it's probably going to be another week before I can see you. I have to cover a few extra shifts in the next week or so, and Maggie is having to adjust her work schedule to take care of the kids." Adam might as well be married to Maggie, since I always ended up like the mistress on the side. Although I understood their relationship and empathized with her plight, I missed my boyfriend. Selfish as it may be, I wanted to come first.

"No problem. There's something I need to talk to you about if you have a minute." Now was the best chance I had to explain the Earl situation.

"I can't now. Gotta go, babe." And he hung up before I could fill him in.

"Who was on the phone?" Spinning around, I gasped when my eyes landed on Earl's damp set of abs and trailed down to the cut of muscle leading to what he was hiding beneath a skimpy towel. "Fuck me," I mumbled.

"That can be arranged." Earl stepped forward, dropping his towel and planted a long, wet kiss on my lips.

CHAPTER 18
ADAM

It sucked having to let Eden go when all I wanted was to hear his voice. Reading a set of instructions would sound sexy from his plump, pink lips. Right now, Maggie needed me more. I'd make it up to Eden in many ways later, enough that he'd forget our time apart.

Maggie wasn't kidding when she said Amber had been having nightmares. I'd been home one night and she'd woken up screaming in terror until I went in the room. Unable to leave her side, since she had a death grip on me, I curled up in bed and fell asleep next to her.

By the time I woke, I'd missed my alarm and two calls from Eden. An hour late for my shift, I downed two cups of horrible hospital coffee when I arrived and promised I'd cover another resident's time since they'd covered me. There went my extra hour to call Eden.

From the time I arrived at work, I was on my feet running. At the end of shift, I had another call from Eden, so I texted him a quick message.

Me: Just got off work, totally wiped. Will talk later. Love you.

Eden: Okay, call me this evening please.

"No I love you back? Wonder if I did something to make him mad?" Thinking out loud, I hoped my time away hadn't made Eden rethink things.

"Make who mad?" Maggie asked, walking up behind me as I got to the front door.

"Eden. His text is a little strange." The few texts we'd sent to each other had always been full of flirting and sexy talk. His text today was to the point and impersonal. Maybe I was reading too much into it.

"Call him and ask." Maggie made everything seem so simple.

"I'm wiped. I'd be no good to anyone in a conversation right now. I'll call him as soon as I wake up this evening." If he were upset with me for spending time with Maggie, my mood now would possibly cause me to snap at him or get annoyed, and I wanted to have a fresh, rested mind before we talked.

Again, I slept straight through the alarm, which was luckily set for an hour early, and was awakened by my phone ringing. These extra shifts were kicking my ass. Hoping it was Eden, I answered, "I've been dying to hear your voice all night."

"Is that sarcasm? Because you actually seem sincere, but I know it's not true." The voice didn't belong to Eden; it belonged to Luann, a nurse at my hospital.

"Shit, I have to come in, don't I?"

"That's more like the response I was expecting. Yep. Dr. Carson is on first call, but I can't reach him, so you're up, sunshine." Luann was one of my favorite emergency room nurses, because no matter what, she always had a sunny disposition and positive outlook on life. I needed her to rub off on me a little.

"I'll get dressed and be right in. Be there in twenty." From the moment I'd heard her voice I'd started hopping around the room searching out my scrubs, sniffing them in hopes that someone had thought to do my laundry. No such luck. Squirting soap over a washcloth, I scrubbed my naughty bits at the sink. With a bottle of Febreze, I spritzed my scrubs from the night before, put on one gray sock and one black one, and ran down the stairs.

Maggie walked into the living room as I ran down the stairs, jumping when I was only three from the bottom. "Where's the fire?" Sniffing the air, she asked, "Is that Febreze?"

"Can you be the best friend ever and do my laundry tonight? I haven't got a clean pair of scrubs to save my life." Snatching the sandwich off her plate, I shouted, "Thanks! Love you!"

"That was my sandwich, jackass!" followed by laughter, was all I heard as I shut the door behind me. It wasn't my first sandwich heist since moving into this house, and wouldn't be my last. Maggie had grown accustomed to my grab 'n' go days when I was on call.

Luann was grinning behind a vase of roses when I walked in the doors. "You've been holding out on me, dear. Who's the lucky guy?"

"You tell me, sunshine. They're for you." A small white card was attached to a plastic stick in the middle of the arrangement. The card read "I hope you know how much you mean to me. Love, Eden."

My night was made. He couldn't be mad at me if he was sending me roses. "My super cute and ubersweet boyfriend, Eden."

Primping the roses, moving around baby's breath, Luann commented, "I assume they're a sweet gesture and not an apology for something he did wrong?"

"Definitely a sweet gesture." Then again, he'd been desperately trying to reach me for the last few days. Could it be possible he'd done something? When I called him my boyfriend the other day, he'd seemed surprised. Maybe he'd been seeing someone else this whole time?

"Everything okay?" Looking up at Luann, I shrugged. "You went from deliriously happy to lost puppy look in less than a minute."

Paranoia got you nowhere in a relationship. I wasn't going to worry about what might be going on until I had a reason to worry. "Just wish I had a desk to display these on, or that they'd come on my way out."

"Delivery guy apologized. Orders were for him to deliver them in the morning, but they got placed on the truck by mistake this evening. You can leave them here. I'll take care of them for you, sweet cheeks."

Plucking a rose from the vase, I gave it a short sniff before handing it over to Luann. "Thanks, Lu. Keep this one for you, doll." Walking toward the charts, I grabbed my phone from my pocket and sent a quick text to Eden.

Me: Got called in to work. I miss you. The roses are beautiful (delivery guy fucked up). I love you. I promise we'll talk in the morning no matter how crazy my shift is.

CHAPTER 19
EDEN

Three days had gone by since I'd spoken to Adam and since Earl kissed me. And I'd said yes to Earl when he asked to stay another day. Why was I such a sucker for him? There were no feelings left between us, I knew that for a fact. Yet somehow, I felt guilty pushing him away.

After the shock of the kiss wore off, I laid things out for Earl. A long conversation ensued about how much I loved Adam and how we could be friends but he couldn't try to make a move or kiss me again.

He took the rejection rather well. Over the last few years, he'd only had one semiserious relationship. Life revolved around him spending time with his mother when he wasn't working. Lack of free time kept him from making friends, which was why he'd called me when life became too hard to bear alone.

Guilt over the kiss ate away at me. I wanted to tell Adam and get it off my chest. His work schedule made it impossible to reach him. Sending roses was a last-ditch effort to let him know I was thinking of him. Earl offered to leave, but I'd seen the fear in his eyes when he talked about being alone. One more day couldn't hurt. Once I talked to Adam, everything would be better.

Although the attraction was gone, the friendship with Earl was still there. We'd stayed up late at night reminiscing about our college days. He'd confided in me about his loneliness over the years. "I know you're ready for me to leave." He stopped me when I began to argue. "You like your space, Eden. Without my mom, I have nothing to go home to but an empty house of things I have to pack up. I know you don't want me here. I can feel the annoyance, but you're the only friend I've got. I promise I'm gone after tomorrow."

"I'm not going to lie. Having you here makes me nervous about my relationship with Adam. And you're right, I love my personal space. However, I couldn't turn away a friend in need."

He wrapped his arms around me, and I felt the emotions spill out from him as he shook in my arms. Being raised Catholic brought a conscience I couldn't ignore, making me feel guilty for thinking of turning a friend away. I needed to have faith in my relationship with Adam.

"I've got two yards on my schedule today. I'll be gone most of the day, but make yourself at home, and we'll have a nice dinner for your last night in town." Leaving Earl at my house felt weird, but unavoidable. My first lawn of the day was for one of Adam and Maggie's neighbors. She'd seen the job I had done on their yard and begged for my number a few months back.

While I was in the vicinity, I planned to stop and say hello to Maggie and scope things out on Adam's schedule for the next few days, since I hadn't been able to ask him myself.

Mrs. Mayfield answered the door in her nightgown, quickly wrapping her arms around herself and blushing when our eyes met. "I'm sorry, ma'am, I'm a little early today. Do you mind if I get started or would you rather I come back?"

"No worries, dear. I'll get dolled up while you work, and then when you come for the check, you can tell me how well I clean up." Blowing me a kiss, she giggled a little and shut the door. Shaking my head, I chuckled, thinking about how much she reminded me of my own grandmother.

Before getting started, I grabbed a bag from my truck containing chopped-up banana peels. Using them as a cheap fertilizer saved me a fortune with my business. At first I was getting tired of eating bananas all the time, but then Eve had a great idea. She asked Jackie's school principal to save their banana peels for me each week. In exchange, I built the bookcases in the library at cost, which was an extreme discount for them.

Quite proud of her rose bushes, Mrs. Mayfield paid me extra to give them special attention. Each week they were given two inches of water, a puree of banana peels mixed with coffee grounds, and once they bloomed, I snipped them and carried a vaseful inside. Those were the most precise instructions ever given to me by a client.

Up to my elbows in dirt, I heard a whistle from a few feet away. "Hi, Eden!" Maggie was jogging across the yard toward me. Even in sweats, with her hair pulled up into a bun, the woman was gorgeous. How she'd stayed single for two years was beyond me.

"Hey, Maggie. Off work today?"

"Yes, sir. Out for a morning jog before going to pick Amber up from her grandparents'. I'll be glad when she starts school in a few months. I'm sure Adam will be too, so he'll have some more time with you." Stopping a few feet from me, she jogged in place, panting with each word, to keep up her rhythm.

The mere thought of more time with Adam had me

giddy with hope. "Adam at work?"

"He got called in early last night. It's getting to him." She didn't elaborate, so I had to ask.

"What is?"

"Not seeing or speaking to you. He's pretty crazy about you, Eden. I haven't seen him this crazy about a guy since…." Her words trailed off, but I knew she meant since Donovan, her late husband. "You'll be over later, right?"

"Of course, it's my day to mow for you."

"Mrs. Mayfield has made Adam so many cookies since he recommended you. Those sexy abs of his may disappear by the next time you see him. And she never stops bragging about her roses." Mentally patting myself on the back, I looked over her roses and smiled at their beauty.

"I need to get back to my jog. See you in a little while," she called out as she sprinted back to the street. Staying healthy was important for me, but jogging was not something I'd ever do intentionally. If a serial killer was chasing me, maybe, but only then.

Finishing up at the Mayfield house, I checked the time. I'd timed things perfectly to catch Adam getting home. Maggie's car was gone, so I started on the yard and would talk to her later.

Two hours later, I was sweaty, grimy, and starving. Adam's car pulled into the driveway, and I watched him look around for me. Suddenly my nerves were on fire. How would he react about the kiss? No matter what happened, it was important for me to tell him before I lost my courage.

"Eden!" he exclaimed when his gaze found me. In a few strides he was in my arms.

"Sorry, I'm sure I smell terrible." Sweat, banana peels, dirt; it would never make a marketable cologne fragrance.

"Oh please, I worked two shifts with not even so much as a whore bath in between, and I'm wearing these scrubs for the second, possibly third time. I febrezed them this morning." Cocking an eyebrow, he asked, "That's my confession, what's yours?"

"What do you mean?" Fear wrapped itself around my heart as it sped up.

"I mean what were the 'forgive me' roses for?" He knew me too well, better than I knew him, because when my eyes fell away from his and my hands dove into my pockets, he said, "Shit. I was kidding, but it seems like I nailed it."

Words had lost all meaning to me as I watched the pain roll across his features. "It's not what you think."

"Eden, don't bullshit me." With a firm jaw and anger in his eyes, he stood waiting.

"I won't, I promise."

"It's not what you think is a complete bullshit

answer!" For the first time since we'd met, Adam raised his voice to me. "I knew you sounded too shocked the other day by me calling you my boyfriend. I should've known this would happen."

"Are you going to let me explain or are you going to act like an asshole?"

"Fuck you, Eden. I guess I'm an asshole. Whoever the guy is you've been fucking behind my back must be a prince. So go home to him." He couldn't even look at me now. His eyes were focused on something in the distance.

"You jumped to that assumption rather quickly. It's nice to know you think I'm such a man whore." Sure, I felt guilty about the kiss, but it was one kiss and nothing more since. It had ended almost before it began. "It was nothing more than a kiss, Adam. And it was him kissing me followed by me pushing him away. Not a big deal, but I wanted no secrets between us."

As I started to leave, Adam called out to me. "Eden, I'm sorry. I—"

"You made an ass out of you and me is what you did. We're done, Adam. I won't be treated like shit by anyone." I kept my composure until I got to the van, but the moment I turned out of the driveway, the emotions took over. Angry, frustrated sobs of heartbreak broke free from my body.

CHAPTER 20
ADAM

When I explained to Maggie what had happened, she reiterated what an ass I'd been. It was hard to argue with her logic. It was also tough to trust at times. If Eden had—no, if *I* had let Eden explain, things would have gone much differently.

Maggie suggested I text him, but it seemed too impersonal. Since I'd taken call for Dr. Carson the other evening, I asked him to take my shift, which he was happy to do. It was my turn for "I fucked up" roses, but I would deliver them in person. Tying a bow around my cock and wearing a raincoat crossed my mind, but I thought I should go for the romantic instead of naughty, considering the situation.

At the florist, I decided flowers were too clichéd for what had happened. Perhaps what I needed to do was get the advice of another person. "Ma'am?" I called to the young lady behind the counter.

Grinning like she'd won the lottery, she peered up at me with wide eyes. "How can I help you, sir?"

"If you got in a fight with your boyfriend and accused him of something he didn't do, how would you apologize?" It was a nicer way to ask than how to correct calling your man a cheating man whore.

"Girlfriend troubles?" Apparently she thought I was using an analogy instead of asking a question.

"Nope, boyfriend." She wasn't fazed, which was good. Living in the Bible Belt, you never knew how people would react.

"Chocolates usually work for me when my boyfriend screws up. We have a pretty nice selection in the back, but I recommend driving down the street to the Godiva store." Stepping around the counter, she led me to another section of the store. "Most people don't know we have gifts as well."

In front of me was a large selection of candles, statues, candies, bath soaps, and lotions. "Sexy time is one of the best ways to say sorry. I suggest a good-smelling candle." Lifting a pale yellow candle to her nose, she closed her eyes as she breathed it in. "Tahitian vanilla makes me happy."

She held it out to me, and I took a whiff. "Pretty nice."

"A few candles, some bath salts, a little lotion, and you have yourself a recipe for a happy night." Wiggling her eyebrows, she bumped her hip against mine.

"Sounds like a good plan to me. Ring it up, and add in a single red rose." The cash register beeped as she scanned each item in. My final total was almost a hundred dollars. It was worth it to give Eden a good night after the way I acted.

Sending a quick text, I let him know I was on my way over to talk. No response seemed better than having him tell me not to come over.

Pulling into the driveway, I developed a nervous stomach, worried about losing this man I'd grown so fond of over a few stupid comments I didn't mean. With a deep breath and little hope in my step, I walked up to the door. I knocked and waited, taking a few more deep breaths for courage. I was glancing down as the door opened, and spotted a pair of bare feet. My eyes trailed upward, taking in muscular calves, a strong set of thighs, and a towel wrapped around hips with a sliver of skin showing almost up to the best parts.

With a grin I peered up, only to lose my footing and step backward when my eyes landed on an unfamiliar male face. "Can I help you?" Thick arms were crossed over a taut chest glistening with drops of water. It was clear he had just finished showering.

"I was looking for Eden." Everything about our conversation came rushing back. Was it possible this was the guy he'd kissed and after our fight he'd run straight into his arms for good?

"He's just finishing up his shower. Long day, ya know?" Giving me a wink, he motioned inside. "Would you like to come inside?"

Ready to lose my lunch all over the front porch, I declined. "Don't you have something for him?" the man asked, looking a bit confused.

"Yeah. You can tell him Adam said I came to apologize but found out there was no need." The mostly naked man's face fell into a look of horror. "From the look on your face, I'm guessing you've heard of me."

"Look, it's not what it looks like." I was so tired of hearing those words. "Seriously, stick around and he can explain everything. My name is Earl."

"Fuck you, Earl." Storming off, I tossed the red rose to the ground, stomping on it as I walked to my car. Why did that name sound familiar? Had he mentioned the man's name before? I wracked my brain trying to remember our talks, but there was only one thought in my mind. Eden had cheated on me.

A hundred dollars down the tube. Guess I wasn't wrong when I accused Eden of not wanting to be with me. All I wanted to do was scream at the top of my lungs and punch the shit out of something. Instead, I sat in my car, feeling the sheer pain of heartbreak. With the best timing ever, Maggie called me.

"Hey, Mags. It didn't go well."

CHAPTER 21
EDEN

After my fight and possible breakup with Adam over a stupid kiss, I went straight home to find Earl napping on my couch. He was quickly becoming the nightmare houseguest comedies are written about. If he didn't leave soon, my happiness would be thrown out the window.

When Adam had tried to apologize, I'd been too hurt to accept it. On the way home, I'd given it a lot of thought and determined I would show up tomorrow after we'd both had some time to think and see if he would talk to me.

"Earl, you seriously need to go home soon." It was supposed to be an under-the-breath mumble, but I sort of shouted it at him instead. It was hard to hold back my emotions.

"You were so happy when you left here. What

happened? Did you miss seeing Adam?" Earl stood and walked over to me, placing his hand on my shoulder.

"Nope. I saw him. He accused me of sleeping around before I could explain to him about the stupid kiss." Noting the look of hurt cross Earl's face, I quickly added, "I'm sorry. It's nothing against you, Earl."

"I could talk to him for you, if it would help?" His sincerity heightened my guilt over telling him to leave.

"I don't think it would help. Thank you for the offer." Shuffling through the papers on my table, I came across a bill from the hospital. "Dammit. I need to call about this. Will you excuse me?"

"Sure. Um, I'll get out of your hair today. Do you mind if I grab a quick shower before I go?"

"Of course not. Help yourself." The shower turned on a few minutes later, and I could barely make out Earl singing as I sat on hold for the billing company. They'd messed up part of the hospital bill, and I needed to have it corrected. Too much of my and Eve's money had gone into that place already.

After dealing with the representative and getting told I had to contact the insurance company instead, I gave up for the day. A strong smell hit my nose and I held my arm up to sniff myself. It was coming from me.

The shower had quit running, so I knocked on the bathroom door. Earl answered wearing only a towel. A few days ago, the sight would have made me drool, but I'd become immune to him. "I need to grab a shower. Can you change in my room?"

"No problem."

"Oh, and if you hear the doorbell ring, will you answer it? I'm expecting a package and I got a notice that it will be delivered shortly." Adam loved my grind and brew coffeepot and had mentioned how much he and Maggie could use one. I had found a great deal on one and ordered it online the other day—before our fight.

"Sure, man, no problem."

"And, Earl, feel free to flirt. My UPS man is quite the hottie." The same guy had been delivering to me for a few years now. We'd flirted back and forth, but it had never gone any further. If I could set Earl up, it'd release some of the guilt I felt.

"Maybe I'll stay in the towel a few more minutes."

"You've become such a man whore." I winked, and we both laughed.

The warm rush of water soothed my skin. Leaning back, I ran my hands over my hair, soaking it and getting rid of any loose grime. Playing in the dirt all day was my job, and I tended to bring my job home.

Adam's face popped into my head. Wanting him

here with me, I took the soap and lathered my skin, pretending his hands were touching me. I ran the soap along my jaw, imagining his mouth making a trail across my neck, gliding over the spot where he'd given me a hickey. Running my hands across my abs, I thought of him stroking himself in front of me, and me removing the bow and replacing it with my mouth.

With a handful of bubbles, I reached down to wrap my hand around my length, making long, lingering strokes. Moaning, I pressed back against the wall. "Adam." His name slipped through my lips in a soft whisper.

I wanted to taste him again. Needed to feel him inside me. Yearned to be skin against skin, writhing naked together under the hot spray. Picking up the pace, I jerked myself off until I had filled my palm with cum.

After washing off, I stepped out and grabbed a towel. In the bedroom, I looked for an outfit to wear and startled when Earl came to the doorway with a sullen expression.

"What's wrong?"

"I answered the door as you asked. I was in my towel. And you were right, the guy who came to the door was hot." His story didn't match the expression on his face.

"So, what's the problem?"

"The problem is that the guy at the door didn't have the package. It was Adam. And he thinks we slept together." The shirt in my hand fell to the floor as fear crushed my chest.

It seemed like I'd never get this worked out. "What did you tell him?"

"As soon as he told me who he was, I said it's not what it looks like. He wouldn't listen though." When Earl had first arrived, I might have expected he would try to come between Adam and me, but I knew that wasn't the case now.

"Yep, that was definitely Adam. Fuck." If he had any flaws, it was jumping to conclusions. As much as I loved the man, I needed him to do better with trusting me. How could we ever make this work if he always thought the worst?

"I promise I tried—"

Raising my hand, I interrupted his apology. "It's not your fault. I need to get dressed and get over there before I lose any hope for a future with him." We'd already lost six months we could have shared together. I knew what I wanted, and without a doubt, it was Adam. If I had to fight like hell to get him back, I'd do it because he was worth it.

"Eden, tell me it isn't true." Maggie answered without a hello when I dialed her number. Calling Adam would've probably begun with harsh hateful words from him—or he wouldn't have answered. Obviously he'd filled Maggie in on what he thought had happened.

"It's not. Adam misread what he saw, I promise you. I need to get him to speak to me somehow, and I know I can't achieve that alone."

"Name a place, I'll get him there. You two belong together. No stupid misunderstanding should get in the way." Again, I completely understood how Adam could love her.

"I don't want to do some grand, romantic gesture with flowers because I think he would walk away before I could explain. Don't you?" I had to rely on Maggie's expertise, since she knew Adam better than anyone.

"You're right." Nails tapping on a hard surface could be heard through my phone. "This may seem a bit crazy, and it will probably be difficult to arrange, but I think I have an idea."

"Difficult and crazy are my forte. Lay it on me, Mags." She chuckled in the phone, most likely due to the fact I had picked up on Adam's nickname for her.

"Donovan and I had a cabin on the lake. I haven't been since he died, but it's secluded and comfy. I told Adam the other day I wanted to go up there again to look through some boxes. He has a day off coming up in a few days. I can get him to the cabin then." A secluded cabin sounded perfect to me.

"A few days is a long time to wait while he thinks I'm a cheating asshole." In truth, a few minutes of him thinking it had torn me apart inside.

"I can try to convince him to go sooner. We'll have to see what his schedule looks like. But in the meantime, I will sing your praises and talk him into giving you a chance to explain."

"I don't know if—"

"Trust me, Eden. I know how to calm Adam. I'll be so convincing that he won't even think about turning around when he sees you at the cabin waiting for him." The confidence in her voice gave me hope I couldn't find on my own.

"Let's do it."

After a lot of thinking about how the next couple of days would go, I decided to send a text to Adam so he'd know I wasn't ignoring what happened.

Me: I heard you stopped by my house. I know it sounds cliché, but it's not what you think. Nothing happened and there is an explanation for everything. When you've had a chance to calm down, can we talk? Please?

After the longest few minutes of my life, my text alert finally sounded.

Adam: Let me have some space. When I'm ready to talk, I'll let you know.

It was enough to let me know we had a chance.

TWO DAYS AFTER I SPOKE TO MAGGIE, SHE SENT ME A TEXT with the address of the cabin. Adam would be there the next evening with a bag packed for two nights. When she made the request for him to go, he called and took two days off work in order to use the time to think things over.

Another text came telling me to meet her in the morning at the Starbucks down the street from her house so she could give me the key. She was wearing a baseball cap and sunglasses, and I barely recognized her when she walked in. "You look like you're in the witness protection program," I teased.

Removing the cap, she shook her hair out with a laugh. "I wanted Adam to believe I was going jogging so I had to look the part." Her key ring had at least ten keys on it. Going straight to a silver one in the middle, she removed it and handed it over. "This will get you in the front door. Make sure you're up there before he is. It's probably a bit dusty."

"Thanks again for everything, Maggie. I hope this works."

"Me too. He's been moping around the house with a broken heart for the last few days. I've been talking you up, but he's still been in a funk. I want him to smile again. I know it's a lot of pressure, but make sure it happens, Eden." I admired their love for one another. I'd never had a friendship so strong with anyone, other than Eve.

"I'll do my very best. His smile is one of the things I love most." We exchanged hugs before she gave me a kiss on the cheek and left.

* * *

ARRIVING AT THE CABIN, I GOT A TEXT FROM MAGGIE that Adam had just left, which gave me an hour to get ready for him. The cabin had a carport in the back. According to Maggie, Adam always kept his car parked in the front when he went there because he hated traipsing through the dark to get in and out of the house. The back porch didn't have any lights around it. Donovan had wanted to put some motion-sensor lights in, but never got around to it.

Outside, the cabin was beautiful and pristine. Inside, the furniture was covered in sheets and there was dust and cobwebs on everything. Before Adam got there, I'd need to do a little sprucing up.

The bedroom at the end of the hall was the master,

but I left it untouched due to the sentimentality of love shared there. Taking over one of the smaller bedrooms, I placed a few candles around the room, dusted and cleaned the furniture, and placed a new comforter on the bed, obtained from the closet in the room.

Just as I was about to sit down to relax, I heard a key turning in the lock. The door opened and Adam strolled in, tossing his backpack to the couch. He looked around the room, and I watched his face, hoping for a smile when he spotted me. "Shit!" His eyes had drifted past me at first, and then it registered and he cursed and fell back a little. "What the hell are you doing here?"

"We need to talk," I replied.

CHAPTER 22
ADAM

It took ten years off my life, seeing Eden lurking in the shadows of the cabin. After the initial shock, I grew angry. "What the hell are you doing here?"

"We need to talk." I hated those words.

"You said you'd let me come to you when I'm ready. I came up here to think things over." Turning back toward the door, I grabbed my backpack and swung it over my shoulder. When I opened the door, Eden jumped in front of me. "I know, I'm sorry. Please, baby, listen to me."

"Baby? You've never called me that before, and don't have your guilt start you on it now." The use of the endearment made my blood boil, as though four simple letters that sounded so sweet rolling off his tongue could make me forget the pain.

"Okay, Adam. Nothing happened with Earl. I want

to tell you everything that's gone on lately, but I need you to stop and listen without jumping to conclusions or leaving before I finish." Rolling my eyes, I was about to deny him when he said, "I know you don't owe me anything, but if any part of you cares about me or ever did, you'll give me a chance to explain."

Damn, he's cute when he's begging, lower lip jutting out in a pout, eyes all big like a sad puppy. "Fine." I tossed my backpack on the couch and lifted a sheet off a chair across from it. Eden sat next to my bag on the couch, which was what I wanted him to do. Close enough to talk, but not touch.

"Earl was my first love. He was the one who made me admit I was gay. We were together for five years." So far his story wasn't giving me hope. Now I remembered hearing the name when Eden told me about his coming out story. "In the end, he was too much of a mama's boy for me. He chose her over me every time." There was so much history between them, I wasn't sure Eden was over him. The story made me more uncomfortable instead of easing my worry. And Earl was built like a rock; Eden had left that part out of his story before. Maybe he'd been afraid it would make me jealous.

"About a week ago, Earl called me. We hadn't spoken in over four years, and for two years before that it was only through Facebook posts."

"What changed?"

"Nothing for me. For Earl, his mom died and he said he needed a friend. I explained to him I thought I was in a relationship, and he promised friendship was all he wanted." After we'd spent four days having sex together, and said I love you, I would've assumed our relationship would be more than a thought, but I let him finish his story. "You'd have to know his personality. He isn't someone who makes friends easily. Plus, I knew his mom. We shared stories, and I understood his loss. Even though I knew his presence could cause strife between us, I couldn't turn him away while he was grieving.

"When he kissed me, I pushed him away, telling him there'd never be anything romantic between us again. He was disappointed, but after a long talk he understood." Either this story had been greatly rehearsed, or Eden was telling the truth. Whatever the case, my resolve was weakening.

"I don't know how anyone could take rejection from you so easily." Hope filled his features as I spoke. "I know I took it hard."

"I never rejected you, Adam. Only let my insecurities keep me away. Earl isn't still in love with me though, not really. Missing his mom made him want to be with someone who knew her too." Even with the image of Earl's towel-covered lower half in my head and the pain of betrayal, I still loved Eden as much as always. The thought of Earl not still loving him seemed impossible to me. Walking away from his house the other day with the thought of never seeing him again had almost broken me.

"Why was he at your house in a towel?" This story was taking too long, and I didn't have the patience to wait for his explanation.

"I let him stay at my house, and after he kissed me, I tried to turn him away. But his grief was still fresh, so I offered to let him stay a little longer. He knew he was grating on my nerves because I like my privacy, but I knew him well enough to know he needed more time. I allowed him to overstay his welcome until he came to terms with what needed to happen in his life."

If the tables had been turned, I'd have kicked Earl out on the spot. Well, that may not be entirely true, because I wasn't completely heartless. Hearing how Eden had taken in a friend in pain, even if it was an ex-boyfriend, made me love him even more. The harsh truth of the matter was it still wasn't enough for me.

Standing, I headed for the door. None of this explained what had happened when I met Earl at Eden's house. "I'm leaving. I'm sure Maggie won't mind if you stay the night."

Eden grabbed my arm gently, pleading with his eyes as he begged me to stay. "A few more minutes."

Instead of waiting for an answer, Eden continued, "Earl let me cry on his shoulder. Not once during his comfort did he attempt another move." Glancing down at Eden's hand still on my arm, I stepped back over to the chair and took a seat again.

"In all honesty, Eden, we never had the talk. Sure, I told you I loved you, but I never said we were exclusive. If you slept with Earl—"

"I didn't! Not since college, years before I ever laid eyes on you." Grunts of frustration followed as he ran his hands through his hair. "From the moment Earl told me he was coming to town, I tried to get in touch with you to let you know. I didn't want there to be any secrets between us. You were working extra shifts, remember we kept missing calls?"

"You could've texted me."

"I needed to know how you'd react to the news. I wanted to be sure you heard my voice when I told you so you would trust in us." He was right, text was such an informal way of communication and could be easily misinterpreted on the emotions of the words.

"Why did Earl act as though you two had sex when I opened the door? He was still in a towel and flirting with me."

"No innuendo intended, I was expecting a package. The UPS guy has delivered to me for years. We'd shared innocent flirtations, and I knew he was gay. I told Earl to flirt with him, thinking maybe they'd hit it off and it would put a smile on his face. He thought you were the UPS guy. I suppose making you think we'd had sex was his not-so-subtle way of letting the UPS guy know he was gay." It seemed almost ridiculous to be mistaken for the UPS man when I wasn't wearing a uniform.

"Earl is pretty hot, are you sure—" I started to say.

"Adam, you're the only one I want."

"Did Earl leave?" If his answer was no, I'd walk out the door right now. When he hesitated, I started to rise.

"Not right away. The day after you met him is when he left. After you left, he offered to come talk to you, but I wouldn't let him. So I called Maggie, and she and I came up with the cabin idea." Getting Maggie involved was what angered me and won me over at the same time. He'd taken the initiative to talk to someone who knew me best in order to get me to listen to him.

"It sort of makes me mad you brought Maggie into this, but I get that based on my previous behavior and how I acted today, you had no choice. But dammit, Eden, I thought we decided we'd be honest with one another after losing six months?" Not telling me about Earl staying with him was still bothering me. No matter how angry I'd been, his explanation had soothed my fears. Looking in his eyes, I believed there had been no betrayal. And all I wanted to do was make up with him.

"I know. Give me a chance. Just one more. You know they say third time is the charm." Sucking his lips between his teeth, he tried to hold back a smile. "Want to know what I was doing while Earl answered the door?"

"You were in the shower. He told me." My hands smacked down on the chair in annoyance as I readied myself to stand.

"Right. But I was thinking of you. In the shower with me, touching me, stroking my cock." His words were making me hard. My hands relaxed, and I adjusted in the chair as I listened to his voice. He sat forward, his voice lowering. "I closed my eyes, leaned against the wall with the hot water dripping over my body, and I jerked myself off pretending it was you. Now, do you want to walk out the door and never see me again, or would you rather make the fantasy a reality?"

His new tactic had been rather convincing. I stood up and grabbed my backpack from the seat next to him. Defeated, he lay back against the couch, covering his face with his hands. When I dropped it to the floor, he glanced up, surprised. I leaned over him, hands on either side of him on the couch. He started to speak, but I covered his mouth with my own.

Fisting my shirt, he tugged me down on top of him. The salty taste of tears coated his lips, soft lips that caressed mine, sucking first on my bottom lip and then gliding his tongue across the top. My cock hardened as his tongue darted in and out of my mouth in a seductive rhythm, mimicking what my cock wanted to do.

"Take off your pants," he ordered. Unzipping my jeans, I slipped them down to my knees. Eden tugged me forward, his mouth covering the top of my cock through my boxers.

"Fuck me," I groaned, ready to come already.

"That's my plan." Slipping me free of my shorts, he took me fully into his mouth. "Lie back," I requested. Freeing me for a moment, he lay back on the couch. Propping above him, I slid myself back in and began to fuck his mouth.

When he tried to reach up to use his hands, I placed them on my ass instead. He massaged my cheeks as I penetrated his throat, the rhythm erotic. His mouth wrapped around me, and he moaned with each thrust. I closed my eyes, savoring the sensations. Eden's mouth was like heaven; the things he did with his tongue were unnatural. He slapped me hard on the ass, and I came, shooting my load clean down the back of his throat.

"It's my turn now. Take my seat and spread your fucking legs." He'd told me he liked to change things up in the bedroom, but I'd never heard him be so demanding before. It was sexy as hell. The words came out hard, but he still had the adorable smile on his face when he said them that showed it was an act. Eden stood as I removed my pants the rest of the way and sat down. Arms wrapped behind my knees, I held my legs in the air and said, "Give me all you've got."

Eden pulled a condom from the pocket of his pants, slipping it over his engorged member as he stared down at me. Squeezing lube onto his palms, he rubbed them together and stroked his condom-covered cock. After a few strokes with his lubed fingers to loosen me up a little, he slid inside me. Starting out slowly, I bucked against him, wanting more until he was pumping ferociously. There was so much power in his thrusts, teamed with desire in his eyes, but I wanted his orgasm to wait. I needed to feel him for longer. When he tensed up, I cried out, "No, not yet. Hold back. I want more."

"Baby, I can't. I'm ready to come inside you." His face was scrunched up in concentration as he tried to hold back the release. As his balls slapped against my ass, I cried out his name. His eyes rolled back in his head as he came.

All I wanted to do was stay on the couch, enjoying the high, but Eden grabbed my hand and said, "Follow me." Down the hall we went, to the first door on the right, which oddly enough was my room when I stayed there. It was fixed up with a romantic ambiance of candles waiting to be lit.

"This is the room they reserve for me. Did Maggie tell you?"

"No, but I knew theirs would be the master, and I didn't want to disrupt that memory. The other bedroom has two sets of bunks in it, so I assumed this was yours."

"Maybe I'm a bunk bed kind of guy. I do like to switch from top to bottom." Eden moved around the room lighting candles. "I think I'm spent for tonight, baby."

"Now who's using the term of endearment?" Eden teased. "I thought we could lie in here and talk by candlelight. It creates a mood."

After the final candle was lit, I tugged him toward me. "You always put me in the mood." And those lips I'd dreamed about since we'd met were on mine again.

Sliding under the covers, Eden curled up against my chest, spreading one leg over mine so our bodies were linked. Wanting to remember this moment, I touched my nose to his hair, breathing him in. No matter what time of day, he always smelled the same. "Why do you always smell like apples, bananas, and coconut?"

"My shampoo is apple scented, I use banana peels

for fertilizer, and I buy coconut sunscreen in bulk due to my job." Scrunching his nose, Eden asked, "Is it a gross combination?"

Nose still pressed to his skin, I closed my eyes. "Eden, nothing about you is gross. I love the way you smell, even the sweaty, dirty, end-of-day smell you have when you come home from work, because it's you." Kissing his neck, I whispered, "I love you. Every inch of you."

"Move in with me, Adam." Eden's request caught me off guard. I couldn't answer. "You don't have to move right away, but as soon as Maggie can do it on her own, I want you to move in with me. Please consider it."

"I'll speak to Maggie as soon as I get home." Pulling him closer, I kissed his forehead. "The next two days are just for us though. Let's not talk about anyone else. Agreed?"

"Agreed." We both slept soundly, never moving away from the other. Waking up next to him in the morning, I smiled to see his face against my chest. If I could wake up this way for the rest of my life, I'd die a happy man.

A soft buzzing sound drew my attention away from him as I searched the room for my phone. My eyes spotted the vibrating creature across the room on the dresser.

Hugging Eden close and rolling him over, I unlinked our bodies and slipped out of the bed to grab my phone. Bat and balls swinging, I walked down the hallway as I answered. "Hey, Mags. It's a little early to be calling me, don't you think?"

"You don't sound too mad at me, that's a plus. And it's ten o'clock in the morning, you lazy bum." Quickly glancing at my phone, I confirmed the time.

"Shit, we slept in."

"We?" I could hear the shit-eating grin on her face through the phone. I knew she was doing her happy dance, hopping from foot to foot with her head swaying back and forth.

"Yes, *we*. You can stop your happy dance now. I can picture it in my head and almost hear the sound of your feet tapping against the hardwood floor." Charlie Brown's holiday anything was a tradition in our little strange family. Snoopy's happy dance was one we all mimicked, but Maggie did the best impression. Whenever she was over the moon, it was her go-to response. It'd been a long time since I'd seen her do it.

"Cut me some slack. I've spared you from the happy dance lately. Besides, I love Eden and think you two are perfect for each other." How could I argue with that?

"He asked me to move in with him." The words

were delivered in a cautious manner, as I wasn't sure what Maggie's response would be.

"And you told him you would, right?" Not the exact response I expected. Silence followed by a guilt trip was what I'd thought would occur.

"What about you and the kids, Mags?" She'd just finished paying off Donovan's hospital bills, and now Amber was starting school. In a way, it seemed she still needed me. But what if all those things actually meant she was ready for me to go? *Maybe I'm so scared of moving forward with Eden, and I'm making excuses to keep from taking the next step.*

"It's time, Adam. You've put your life on hold for me the last two years. I can't thank you enough for all you've done. The best way for me to thank you is to let you go. And to prove it to you, I accepted a date from a guy at work. His name is Quinton."

"I'm so proud of you, Mags." I knew Donovan would have been happy for her. She'd been alone for too long. A woman so beautiful inside and out deserved to be loved by a great man. "Thank you for helping Eden open my eyes. Our night was spectacular. I'll break the news to him as soon as he wakes up. I love you, Mags."

CHAPTER 23
EDEN

Waking up without Adam was not how I expected my morning to start. My heart skipped a beat when I heard his voice coming from the other room. My smile faded as I stepped out into the hallway and heard him say, "I'll break the news to him as soon as he wakes up. I love you, Mags." I feared the worst, understanding how Adam had felt after our last few fights.

"Break what news?" I asked, fearful of the answer, but desperate for closure of some kind. If Adam couldn't commit to me, I wanted to know now.

Naked as the day he was born, Adam turned to face me. Loving the view, I hoped the news wouldn't taint it. "Maggie called to check on us. I told her you wanted me to move in."

"She begged you to stay?" I glanced down, preparing for heartbreak.

"The opposite. She practically begged me to leave. So I hope the offer still stands, because I'm going to move in as soon as you want me to." I went from defeated to elated in less than ten seconds. Adam seemed quite pleased by my reaction. "I was wondering if I could make one more request, though, before we move in together."

There was a gleam in his eye and a spring in his step. I closed the distance between us and took his hand in mine. "What is your request?"

"Agree to marry me? Not before we move in or even in a couple of months, but I just want you to promise we'll get married at some point. I want you to be my fiancé." Taking a knee in front of me, he waited for my answer. "Please, Eden, marry me?"

"With all my heart I love you, Adam Simmons. Yes, I will marry you." I fell to my knees in front of him and pulled his face forward until our lips crashed together. We sealed the deal not only with a kiss, but by having sex right there on the hallway floor.

The rest of the day was spent in bed. "It's so peaceful here. Besides Maggie's call, our phones have been silent, and there's no outside noise either." Adam's fingers trailed across my skin as he spoke, sending shivers down my spine. "Growing up in the city, working in a trauma department, life has always been loud and busy. It's been a long time since I took a reprieve in this lake house."

"Why do you keep this house if none of you want to visit anymore?" It seemed like a large drain of resources to hold on to if Adam lived with Maggie to help financially. "Couldn't it help with the money issues?"

"The house was purchased by Donovan as a wedding present to Maggie. It was a weekend getaway for them when life got too hectic. They came up here all the time before the kids were born. After number two came along, they started coming back as a family." I could see the joy in his eyes when he talked about the house and what it meant to him. Though there was a bit of sadness mixed in, it was obviously a happy place for him.

"Maggie hasn't been here since he passed?"

"She tried once. Halfway up she turned back around and came home. It's been a hard time for her. Being at the house they shared is one thing, but coming here represents something more personal."

"Do you ever think about moving out of the city?" I grew up surrounded by noises, airplanes flying over, smog, and constant traffic.

"It's crossed my mind. Mags and I keep things light at home, it's why I act immature sometimes. In my job, I see too many injured children and too much death.

Living near a lake, surrounded by trees, having a peaceful place to lay my head, sounds like a dream. But it's a dream for the future. Right now, I could never live too far from Mags." Sitting up, Adam placed his palm against my chest and gazed into my eyes. "I hope you understand. It's not as if I'm choosing her over you. It's not the same as it was with Earl. She loves you and wants us to be together. But she's my best friend and she still needs me."

Placing my hand over his, I lean forward to capture his lips. "I understand better than you know."

CHAPTER 24
ADAM

FOUR YEARS LATER

Today is our three-year wedding anniversary. A year after I proposed, Eden and I married in a simple ceremony in Maggie's backyard. Amber, the shrieking wonder, was our ring bearer, Maggie was my best man, and Eve was Eden's. Nothing traditional about our wedding—or our relationship, for that matter. Donning a white suit and black tie, I was the opposite of Eden in a black suit with a white tie. Our wedding party wore red and the pictures were spectacular with the arrangement of colors.

Today we're celebrating another special occasion on this date. Signing adoption papers for a three-year-old baby girl. Last week when we met her, we fell instantly in love. Eve and Maggie both had offered to surrogate for us, which was an amazing gift, but we chose to give someone a home who was already in need.

"Adam, Eden, I'd like to introduce you again to your daughter. Ms. Madelyn." At first, Madelyn clung to the woman we'd been working with at the agency. We'd picked up a doll for her, along with toys that filled the second bedroom of our new house. Pulling the doll out of the chair next to me, I held it out for her.

"I brought you a doll, Maddie." Thumb in mouth, dark hair in pigtails, she stumbled forward to take hold of the doll.

She grinned up at me. "Dolly."

I held my hands out, hoping she'd let me pick her up. She eagerly raised her arms up to me. I lifted her onto my lap. "At home, we have a lot more toys to show you. Are you ready to see them?" Madelyn nodded enthusiastically.

Tears in his eyes, Eden leaned down and kissed her forehead. "I love her so much already. How is that possible?" Knowing exactly how he felt, I had no reasoning for it. For new mothers who gave birth, there was always a bond, but we'd thought it would take longer with adoption. For some it may, but for us it was an instant connection.

The first few weeks with Madelyn were rough. She slept about as much as a newborn would. Most nights she awoke screaming, unsure of her surroundings.

After the first few nights, I refused to leave her side, setting up an air mattress on the floor of her room. Eden argued with me, wanting to give her a chance to cope, but he lost the fight when he saw her lip poked out and face covered in tears. In the middle of the night, I felt him crawl onto the air mattress beside me. "I missed you," he whispered in my ear.

Three weeks of sleeping on the floor had taken a toll on our backs and our sex life. We needed a night to ourselves. I called in a favor, and Maggie was ecstatic when I asked if she could babysit Madelyn for the night. Since Quinton had moved in with her a year ago, she could leave him at her house and stay at ours.

She gave us the keys to the cabin, and we drove up to the spot where I had proposed, where our relationship had taken the next big step. We'd only been up there one other time since. Maggie went up to see it a year later for a weekend away with Quinton. Upon her request, we drove up early and switched the beds out between the master and my room so she could sleep on a different bed with him than she did her late husband.

Nothing else was different. Sheets still covered the furniture, dust coated the sheets. "It feels like we've come full circle by being here." Eden grinned, looking around. "We should move here."

"Are you insane? It would be an hour commute to work for me." Working days now linked my schedule up with Eden's, but adding an hour drive would cause us to lose some of the extra we gained. With Madelyn in our life now, I wanted more, not less.

"Hear me out. I've been checking around and there's a clinic nearby needing a full-time doctor. As for my landscaping company, I can find work. Or I can do more with my carpentry business. It would mean time at home with Maddie, time for us." Eden's plan sounded like a dream, but it came out of nowhere.

"What brought this up?"

"One of the businesses I've made rocking chairs for, a country-themed restaurant, just offered me a contract to make the furniture for their stores in Tennessee. It would be enough money to live on for a while, even if I never mowed another yard." Reaching into his back pocket, he pulled a roll of papers out and handed it to me. "It's a two-year contract. After it ends, if they don't renew, I can go back to landscaping. Maddie will be in school by then too. What do you think?"

"Maggie wants to sell the lake house?"

"No. The one down the road is for sale. It's a little bigger than Maggie's, and it has a large garage in the back I could use for my workshop. I asked the realtor if we could look at it while we're here. She's waiting for my call. You give me the word."

Planting myself into a chair, I released an audible sigh. When I moved out of Maggie's, it had been hard to be away from the kids and my best friend, but I grew used to it. With Quinton in her life now, I didn't need to be there as much. It seemed a perfect time to make our dream of a peaceful new beginning come true.

"Let's go see it."

In less than an hour, we were standing on the front porch of the lake house for sale. It was two stories instead of one like Maggie's. The backyard had a large two-story garage to match. Eden pointed out how he'd use the garage itself as a workshop and the upstairs room could be a playroom for Maddie. Once we stepped inside the house, I knew exactly what my decision would be.

We walked around, looking at the stone fireplace with cedar mantle in the living room. Hands gliding across the smooth cedar, Eden grinned widely. I followed him down the hallway to the master bedroom, and my mouth dropped open in awe. Beautiful wood paneling filled the room, with a large jacuzzi in the corner. The master bath had a six-by-six walk-in shower with multiple heads for a waterfall effect.

The kitchen was immaculate, with marble counters and dark wood cabinets. "Can we even afford this place?" I whispered to Eden. Pulling out his phone, he typed in the amount they were asking. "Why so low? Is it filled with asbestos or were people murdered here?"

Chuckling low, Eden whispered, "No. The owner wants out. It's been too much to keep up. They're asking what they owe plus a third of what it's valued. What do you think so far?"

"Can we have a minute alone?" I called out to the realtor standing a few feet away talking on her phone. She nodded before stepping out of the room. "Let's do it. Even if I can't get the job at the clinic, let's do this."

"Are you sure?"

"I want to be wherever you are. And the look on your face when we saw this place told me you want to be here, meaning I do." Taking a moment to kiss my husband in what could possibly be our new home, I pulled him into my arms. "Madelyn will love it here too."

"I love you, Adam." Eden kissed my nose. "And don't get mad, but I already submitted your résumé to the clinic, and they are extremely interested in meeting you." Grimacing, Eden closed his eyes, most likely expecting a scolding from me. Instead, I embraced him. "You're not mad?"

"Not at all. I'm excited about our future. As long as I'm with you, I'm happy."

CHAPTER 25
EDEN

Moving day came and it was bittersweet. Eve, though no longer a single mom, struggled with the thought of me living so far away. After showing her the house and Maggie offering to let her use the lake house down the road anytime, she came to terms with it. Eve had been married a year now. That, combined with knowing Maggie had moved forward in her life, told me it was time for Adam and me to take charge of our own lives instead of focusing everything around Eve's and Maggie's.

Packing up our condo had been easy. Saying goodbye to everyone we loved was the part that sucked royally. It was only an hour drive, and we could see each other often, but it wouldn't be the same. Starting up the moving truck, I glanced in the mirror to see Adam hugging Maggie. He swiped his thumb across her eyes, wiping away the tears. Giving her a kiss on the cheek, he hugged her one more time. I watched as he hugged each kid goodbye, and then Quinton. As protective as he was of Maggie, Adam had loved Quinton from the moment he met him. It made our living together much smoother when their relationship grew serious.

Eve had come over the night before to say her goodbyes. She'd promised to take advantage of Maggie's invitation soon. Her husband, Justin, was a good man. Knowing she had him gave me comfort in living far away. Jackie was crazy about him. In fact, she called him Dad, and he'd adopted her as a wedding gift to Eve. All our lives were on track. What a difference four years could make! Life without Adam was impossible to imagine, especially now that our daughter had grown comfortable with us. She called me Daddy and called Adam, Dadam. She came up with the name herself; I think it was after hearing me call him by name so much. The first time she said it, it stuck.

Driving the truck, I kept Adam in sight in the rearview. He stayed close behind, and we talked on the phone the entire way through Bluetooth. Madelyn could be heard singing in the background. Her sweet voice made it hard to be sad about leaving our family behind. We'd see them soon enough, with the holidays being so close.

Christmas was in two months. Everyone would be coming up to stay between the two lake houses to celebrate the holiday. In the meantime, Adam and I would get everything moved in and decorated. The day Adam went to interview for the position at the clinic, they offered him the job. He would be running it himself with several other doctors treating it as a satellite office for their specialties. He took a slight pay cut, but nothing too drastic. The hours made up for any loss of pay. Adam would have regular daytime hours with nights free, and most weekends too, except for taking call once a month.

Week two in the house, we had unpacked the last box, excluding what would be left in storage for now. Adam and I plopped down on the couch next to each other. Intertwining our fingers, I lifted his hand and gave it a kiss. "Madelyn's asleep. The last box is unpacked. Whatever should we do now?" Wiggling my eyebrows, I waited for Adam's response.

"I'm exhausted. If I can get up from this couch and make it to the bedroom, it would be a miracle."

Sighing in relief, I replied, "Oh thank God. Me too. Let's sleep here tonight?"

"Deal." Scooting with very little effort, I then lifted my leg over Adam to rest behind him. He turned to lie against me, his head resting on my chest. "Thank you, Eden, for everything. For the house, the job, our daughter, for being you. I love you."

"I love you more, Adam." Twisting his neck, he gave me a quick kiss. "And I love our life." Together we drifted off to sleep, wrapped up in the comfort of our new life.

THE END

ACKNOWLEDGMENTS

Thank you to my husband who puts up with me writing during every spare minute I have, even if it means he gets ignored. For letting me bounce ideas off him and having the courage to tell me when something seems stupid, as well as for his compliment when I've hit gold with a scene. For this book especially, I appreciate him answering all my questions regarding how male anatomy feels without looking at me as though I was crazy. For him I always put nerd-related moments in my books. He is the one who suggested I write my first novel, the person who has literally been there from day one of my writing and has encouraged me every single step of the way. And the one who tells people I'm an author because I tend to be too shy to talk about it. I love you, Daniel.

Thank you to Hot Tree Publishing for having faith in my writing and believing in my writing and helping to make me grow as a writer with each new release.

Many thanks to Becky and Justine—two of my favorite people in the book community. They have not only helped me for many years but have supported so many authors in the industry; there's no way to thank them enough.

I owe a debt of gratitude to my mom who has read every book I've written and supported me on this venture from the minute I confessed to writing my first book.

To the readers who have been there with me from the beginning to the new ones I've picked up along the way, your encouragement and love of my books keeps me going.

ABOUT THE AUTHOR

Amy K. McClung was born in Nashville, TN. She is the second oldest of four girls and occasionally suffers from middle child syndrome.

She met the love of her life online in August of 2004, on his birthday of all days, and married him in September 2005. Currently they have no human children only the room full of colourful robots that transform into vehicles and the large headed Pop Funko's who represent their favourite characters. Collecting movies, shotglasses, Pop Funkos, and dust bunnies are some of her favourite pastimes.

She began writing in September of 2011 and independently published her first YA novel called Cascades of Moonlight, Book one of the Parker Harris series the following May. Her first book was a means of therapy for her as it enabled her to escape reality for a while during a difficult transition in her life.

facebook.com / AmyKMcclung

twitter.com / AmythaMcclung

instagram.com / amykmcclung

bookbub.com / profile / amy-k-mcclung

ABOUT THE PUBLISHER

Hot Tree Publishing opened its doors in 2015 with an aspiration to bring quality fiction to the world of readers. With the initial focus on romance and a wide spread of romance subgenres, Hot Tree Publishing has since opened their first imprint, Tangled Tree Publishing, specializing in crime, mystery, suspense, and thriller.

Firmly seated in the industry as a leading editing provider to independent authors and small publishing houses, Hot Tree Publishing is the sister company to Hot Tree Editing, founded in 2012. Having established in-house editing and promotions, plus having a well-respected market presence, Hot Tree Publishing endeavors to be a leader in bringing quality stories to the world of readers.

Interested in discovering more amazing reads brought to you by Hot Tree Publishing? Head over to the website for information:

www.hottreepublishing.com